I0621122

Unpopular Opinions

Unpopular Opinions Book Series, Volume 1

Taseef Farook

Published by Unfiltered Ink, 2025.

Table of Contents

Prologue..1

Chapter 1. Unscripted...5

Chapter 2. Delusion or guilt?..29

Chapter 3. Passed away...41

Chapter 4. Uprooted..53

Chapter 5. Generosity..71

Chapter 6. The help... 101

Chapter 7. Alone 121

Chapter 8. Return to sender... 141

Chapter 9. All I have 173

Unpopular Opinions 2... 189

Copyrights page

UNPOPULAR OPINION

By Taseef Farook

ISBN (paperback): 978-1-7638775-2-8

ISBN (Ebook): 978-1-7638775-0-4

Copyright © 2025 by Taseef Farook

All rights reserved.

No part of this book may be reproduced, stored in a retrieval system, or transmitted in any form or by any means: electronic, mechanical, photocopying, recording, or otherwise, without the prior written permission of the copyright holder, except for the use of brief quotations in a review.

The story, all names, characters, and incidents portrayed in this production are fictitious. No identification with actual persons (living or deceased), places, buildings, and products are intended or should be inferred.

Published by **Unfiltered Ink**

Adelaide, South Australia, 5000, Australia

Email: taseef@live.co.uk

Cover © 2025 by Taseef Farook

Unfiltered Ink is an imprint of Dr Farook Ink.

Dedication

To my mother, who instilled in me the value of perseverance and the resolve to see every goal through to the end.

Preface

I am an academic researcher and dentist with a unique cross-cultural perspective, having lived in Bangladesh, Malaysia, and Australia. My diverse background shapes the themes of this novel, as my experiences across these cultural landscapes deeply influence my writing. While all the characters in this story are entirely fictional, their struggles reflect real, systemic flaws in our society—issues that are often difficult to discuss. I believe that humour and wit provide the best way to navigate such sensitive topics, making them more accessible without diminishing their importance.

This book is my attempt to bring these stories to life, inspired by the many people who once shared their experiences with me and the lessons I have learned along the way. It is not written to criticise, but rather to highlight how far we have come and what still needs to change. Merging so many narratives into the voices of two protagonists was no small task, and I am deeply grateful to my partner, Lameesa Ramees, and my good friend, Ragib Farhat Hasan, for helping me weave it all into a singular, compelling story. I couldn't have done it without you.

Finally, I would like to thank Artificial Intelligence (AI) for proofreading my work. Yes, English is not my first language, and as a first-time author without the backing of a major publishing house, I couldn't afford a team of copyeditors.

Blank page

UNPOPULAR
OPINIONS

Prologue

I just finished tying a noose to my bedroom ceiling fan. Did the first line grab your attention? Did you think, "Oh no, please don't!" or maybe, "Good riddance!"? They say the world thrives on shock value these days—all flash and barely any substance. A friend of mine, who proudly lists "Social Media Influencer" on their résumé, swears by clickbait to hook people. Don't worry, I'm not planning to end my life. I only set this scene to prove a point: not all clickbait works, and often, people don't care about a person they don't personally know—just their story, if it's any good. So, no, I'm not going anywhere. Not until I've told you my story, at least.

Okay, here I am, sitting in front of my computer with a blank Word document titled "Thesis chapter 1" open, yet my attention is completely absorbed by a very particular diary in my hands. The green faux-leather cover is worn, its edges frayed, and faint water stains scattered across its surface. This diary had certainly seen better days. I'm unsure whether I should open it and read its contents. Despite my upcoming PhD submission deadline, I find myself more focused on the diary than on my thesis. But for my predicament to make sense, I'll need to give you some context.

Let me take you back to a year ago. Imposter syndrome had just begun creeping into my mind as I embarked on my second year of the PhD journey. For those unfamiliar, imposter syndrome in academia is a dark cloud of doubt. It's when a researcher starts questioning the value of their work, and in the process, begins questioning their entire existence—a kind of existential crisis. And yes, it's practically a rite of passage for doctoral candidates. Often, it comes paired with vivid flashbacks of every questionable decision you've ever made in life, including the one that led me to my counsellor's office in the first instance.

And no, it's not karma for all the "helpless" animals you think we scientists kill for fun in the name of research. Let me assure you, getting ethical approval for even the simplest experiment involving another life is a harrowing process that can take years. No one is submitting an ethics application saying, "We're planning to stab a thousand sheep to see if they all bleed the same," only to wait indefinitely for a rejection letter from the ethics committee that might arrive on our deathbed. It just doesn't work like that!

I was in my university's appointed mental health counsellor's office. There I was, sitting across from my counsellor, an exceptionally patient man who listened to me pour out why I've been beating myself up, why I think this grief is rearing its head now, right when my PhD has hit a low point.

"I just got back from Bangladesh after spending the final hours with a loved one," I began hesitantly, "and now I've inherited their diary. I don't know if I should read it."

My counsellor tilted his head, considering. "That sounds like a very simple, though immensely personal, dilemma. Why did you feel the need to come and see me for that?"

I took a deep breath, my voice faltering slightly. "I'm terrified about what I might find. He was my closest friend, and he was with me during a time when... 'certain' things happened. I'm scared of what he might have seen and written."

My counsellor readjusted his position in his chair before continuing. His tone was calm but probing. "Is there something in your past that is still bothering you?"

I shifted uncomfortably realising how his generic observation cut too close. "Maybe," I admitted, "but it's the diary that's bothering me. I was fine—well, I thought I was—until it ended up in my hands. Now, I can't stop thinking about a certain time in my life, but I don't think that's relevant."

He raised an eyebrow but didn't push. "I'd still like to hear your story first, if you're okay sharing it."

I hesitated, then nodded. And in what felt like an instant, an hour had passed. It's funny how easy it is to pour your heart out when the counselling service is free, courtesy of the university. I didn't even notice that I hadn't looked at my counsellor the whole time, just talking aimlessly, as though everything that had been buried inside for years was spilling out. This wasn't some movie scene with a plush red divan and a patient dramatically covering their face, staring at the ceiling, while a therapist scribbles notes. I was perched on a stool, while my counsellor sat across the room. No fancy note-taking, no close proximity—just an ocean of distance between us, maybe for social distancing or maybe to give him room in case I lunged at him with the sharp blade of my emotions!

I talked about everything—my childhood, the moments that had shaped me, and how they had all led me to this point. When I finally glanced up at my counsellor, he looked exhausted. His eyes were wide, his eyebrows raised, and a mix of disbelief and confusion played on his face.

I couldn't help but ask, "Was it that bad? Do I need therapy?"

He smiled slightly and said, "I don't think it's bad. But I do think you should write a book. It would make for a great read."

I laughed. "You mean my PhD thesis?"

"No," he said gently. "Your life story...A memoir of sorts! Share what you feel comfortable sharing—like what you just told me, and all those things you've kept buried for so long. I think it's important you come to terms with your side of the story first, before diving into someone else's—especially someone so close to you. Otherwise, you risk losing perspective."

I laughed nervously. "Don't you think I'm a little too young to be writing a memoir?"

He smiled and said, "It doesn't need to be a memoir. It just simply needs to be an account of how things were through your eyes. And from what I've heard so far, I think you've already lived through more than most people do in a lifetime. Trust me, your story will make for a compelling read."

I nodded, still uncertain. "But what about Sufi's diary?"

He chuckled softly. "The diary can wait, Yaad. My priority is counselling the living, not the departed. I doubt your late friend will benefit much from it. Once you've finished writing your own story, we can go through the diary together, step by step."

I nodded. My counsellor glanced around the room, then checked his wristwatch and said, "Looks like we're out of time today. I should ask management to get something to tell the time for the office."

I thanked him for his time. As he stood, scratching his head as if searching for the right words, he added, "Give us a call to book another session whenever you're ready to talk again."

And here I am, a year later, writing my story while still wrestling with the decision of whether to read Sufi's diary. So, let's take a brisk walk down memory lane together. While I have the habit of occasionally procrastinating and going off topic, I'm not one for slow burns or dragging out the buildup so I promise to keep this story fast-paced.

I've already started thinking like an academic, planning to publish my life story before I've even written it. *Publish or perish*, right? Just so we're clear: I can't promise my story will teach anyone how to do their taxes or get out of debt, nor is it the memoir of some celebrity with famous friends praising a book they've probably never even read. There's no stampede of literary agents or overzealous press ready to blow my story out of proportion, and no marketing team slapping on clichéd, one-word reviews like "breathtaking," "brilliant," or "must-read." But what I can promise you is this—I have a story. And it's a good one.

Anyway, I'll take you on a journey to show how I got to where I am today and what exactly raised my counsellor's eyebrows.

Chapter 1. Unscripted

Let me tell you a bit about myself, first. I love traveling, socialising, and diving into video games—especially those that let me immerse myself in worlds where every decision shapes the outcome. Yes, I'm one of those who fell in love with *"The Witcher"* games without ever picking up Andrzej Sapkowski's books. Games like *"Mass Effect"*, *"Divinity"*, and *"Baldur's Gate"* pull me in because they let me control the story, giving me the power to reload and rewrite choices I'm not happy with. In real life, though, I'm not about to willingly go paragliding off an active volcano—my risks are more calculated, grounded in practical lessons I've picked up along the way that help me live with the choices I've made.

Why is any of this relevant, you might wonder? Well, I wasn't always this way. Once upon a time, I had a naive view of the world. That was before I stumbled across deeply unsettling family secrets—revelations that flipped my life upside down. I saw firsthand the harsh realities of poverty, desperation, and what people do when pushed to their limits. But before we dive into that chapter, let me show you what life was like before everything changed.

I grew up in "Uttara" on the outskirts of Dhaka city, the bustling capital of Bangladesh. We take pride in being home to the largest delta in the world, boasting one of the longest coastlines, and one of the fastest growing economies in the eastern hemisphere. For every flaw in my country, I believe there are two redeeming qualities, though I may be biased. My childhood home was situated in an area where people had just begun settling in the early '90s. In 1996, my family rented a decent-sized, one-story house with a large front driveway and an unfinished second floor that eventually became a makeshift roof. The house was surrounded by a high perimeter wall, with two sides facing beaten dirt roads and the back opening into a stretch of woods. The perimeter gate divided the large driveway in half. I'll describe the layout in

5

more detail when it matters, though I don't see much point in mentioning which section of the wall the villagers favoured as their public bathroom. Yes, people there relieved themselves in public and on other people's properties, but unlike here in Australia, they didn't have to get drunk to do it.

As flawed as the house and its surroundings were, it was home. Outside of school, it was my entire world.

I wasn't allowed to interact with the local children outside of school, nor was I ever permitted to play outdoors. My father forbade it, and when I asked why, his answer was always, "Because I said so!" He'd claim he was worried about my safety, but it always felt like there was more to it than that—something unspoken that went beyond simple concern.

I thought he was always very grumpy, and he had a slight hunch that made him look even more irritable. My mother would occasionally sneak me out, but those adventures often led to fierce arguments between my parents that sometimes escalated to my father scolding my mother in front of me. It's strange how a child's mind works, subconsciously crafting ways to protect loved ones by making sacrifices they don't even realise they're making.

After one too many arguments, I started telling my mother I wasn't interested in going out to play, hoping to spare her the pain that often followed. Instead, I'd run up to the roof and lean over the concrete railing, watching the other kids play in the open areas nearby. I'd watch the occasional car or rickshaw pass by, though back then, it was a rare sight. The roads weren't developed enough to handle much traffic, so vehicles were few and far between. As dusk approached, my mother would call me downstairs, warning me of the terrible mosquito problem caused by the open sewage systems that ran next to our home—nothing could be done about that.

Bored yet? I wouldn't blame you if you were. My life wasn't particularly interesting. The only real communication I had outside of school came from my observation sessions on the roof and the video games I played on an old television screen with my mother. She wasn't great at most games, but she was all I had.

What she truly excelled at, though, was chess, and she was the one who taught me how to play. She always said, "You don't need a college degree to play chess, you just need to be adaptable to change and know how to plan ahead based on that." She also told me that it was often the most unconventional moves or pieces that won the game. People tend to focus on the strongest units, like the queen, when they move, often overlooking the humble knight, which can be just as dangerous when positioned correctly.

Every morning, as I prepared for school, my gaze would inevitably drift toward the grated windows overlooking our front driveway that extended beyond the gated perimeter walls. There, without fail, sat a homeless man, hunched and frail, begging for alms with his back facing towards the window. He was old, his body gaunt and malnourished, draped in a tattered shawl that barely shielded him from the elements. Though his back was stooped and his movements slow, his voice had a beauty that belied his appearance. He would sing, not for the joy of it, but as a way to raise enough money for a scrap of food to sustain him another day.

I can't remember exactly when he first appeared, but as a child, his presence became a constant in my morning activities. His songs fascinated me, although I did not understand a word of what he sang! I'd tug on my mother's sleeve, asking for a penny each morning before she took me to school. It was a small offering, something a child could easily spare. Every time I placed that penny in his hand, he would smile—a smile that seemed both grateful and knowing, as if he understood that a penny wouldn't buy him much. Still, he accepted it, and I found joy in the brief interaction. My mother, noticing how drawn I was to the man, began preparing extra food for him, meals that would last him a day or two. Some of our neighbours did the same, contributing what little they could to help him through another day. My father never objected to his presence.

I didn't particularly enjoy school, but more on that later. What I did enjoy was my journey to school, knowing that I would see him in the morning. At first, by the time I returned home in the afternoon, he would be gone, likely having used his morning's earnings to buy food. His spot on the driveway would be empty, but I knew he'd be back the next day.

As the months passed, however, I began to notice changes, subtle at first. His singing, once rich and melodic, became strained. His voice grew weaker, losing the beauty that had first drawn me in. He was getting thinner too, the lines on his face deeper, his eyes duller. Soon, he didn't have the strength to take the penny from my hand, and his once warm smile disappeared, replaced by exhaustion. Instead of reaching out, he placed a small bowl in front of him, allowing passersby to leave their alms without requiring him to move.

The bowl, which had once filled quickly, now sat half-empty for much of the day. And as his health worsened, so too did his ability to leave. Where he once vanished after collecting enough for a meal, now he remained on our driveway well into the afternoon, his body too weak to go any further. His hearing deteriorated to the point where he couldn't hear someone calling him from just a few feet away and had to be physically tapped to get his attention. I'd come home from school, and there he would be, hunched in the same spot, staring at the empty streets with his bowl barely touched.

Sometimes, the community-appointed security guard from our neighbourhood would ride up on his bicycle and remove him from our driveway. They claimed that begging wasn't welcome in such a place, but my mother and I always found him a few houses away and brought him back. My mother would give him what little food we could afford and even fresh clothes from time to time. I think we were all he had left.

Life on the outskirts of Dhaka had its own rhythm. Our house, while close to the city, bordered rural farmlands, where families lived simple lives. Many of the farmers' wives worked as maids and helping hands in the city to supplement their income. One such woman, known by the locals as "Jahanara's Ma"—or JM, as she'll be referred to for the remainder of this chapter—became a regular visitor. She connected us with young farmers' wives seeking work as maids in exchange for food and some money. Occasionally, we hired one or two to help around the house. They had the option to stay with us in the makeshift attic space leading to the roof, or work only during the day and leave before sunset. Most of these women liked my mother and chose to stay, and since my mother trusted JM, she ensured that those recommended were properly vetted for our safety.

JM had a daughter named Jahanara—*obviously!*—who tragically died in a fire while cooking outdoors. A stray flame caught her clothes, and in seconds, she was engulfed. The story was horrific, and my mother's heart ached for JM. But their connection grew beyond shared grief and quickly became very good friends. In a cruel twist of fate, the locals never stopped calling her "Jahanara's Ma," even after her daughter's passing. It was as if every mention of her name served as a painful reminder, keeping the wound fresh, forcing her to relive that unbearable loss with every conversation. I'm certain most didn't even know her real name!

JM would visit us regularly, bringing fresh vegetables from her farm as a kind gesture. She would spend hours chatting with my mother, sharing stories and laughter while I listened quietly, playing in the background. My mother never completed college and got married to my father at a very young age. She was a welcoming individual, and we kept the gates open when JM joined us, allowing other villagers to join in the conversation occasionally. Uttara was just beginning to develop, with estates and houses like ours springing up amid stretches of woods, displacing open lands as farmers and poorer families chose to sell. Many of these farmers were undereducated and unaware that they were living illegally on land their forefathers had occupied decades ago, now being forced to leave by the new owners drawn to the area as it became a hotspot for the wealthy and retired.

What were we doing there? That's a good question. I didn't have a say in where we lived, so I'll let you read on and draw your own conclusions.

While my five-year-old world revolved around the old man on the driveway and the games I played with my mother, these visits added a layer of warmth and companionship to our otherwise mundane household.

One October afternoon, I was on the driveway, playing with my imaginary friends, as JM walked past. She glanced at the old man, her eyes filled with pity, knowing there was little she could do for him. My mother was inside, waiting for her visit. That day, as they talked, I overheard my mother say, "Yaad has been insisting that I get him a pet chicken!" That was my cue. I rushed over, filled with excitement, and said, "Yes, please!" JM laughed and asked, "Any colour preference?" Without hesitation, I replied, "Anything that clucks!" They both chuckled before returning to their conversation. To this day, I still am unsure as to why I wanted a pet chicken as a child.

A month passed. It was now November, and school was off for the holidays. JM arrived at our house again, this time with her husband and several chickens in tow. She insisted I take them all for free, but my mother only allowed me to take one, on the condition that I pay for it with my daily penny allowance. Excited, I handed over the penny, the same penny I had been giving to the old man for nearly a year. It was a hard choice, but I chose the chicken. I didn't know what I'd do with it, but convincing my mother to get me a chicken was already a victory.

As I paid JM, I glanced over at the old man as he sat in his usual spot. Only this time, he didn't try to sing. He was silent, his shawl torn, his clothes stained with spots of blood. My mother turned to JM and asked, "What do you think happened to him?" JM's husband replied,

"Could be anything. The railway shelter and the surrounding shanty has stray dogs, and the people there can be violent. He could've been attacked." The conversation was cut short when the old man, now using a walking stick, got up and hobbled away.

Later that day, my mother asked JM and her husband to build a small coop for the chicken behind our house, away from my father's sight. I begged to let the chicken sleep with me in my room, but my mother firmly said no. Despite her refusal, I wasn't too upset. I had a whole week of school holidays left to play with my new pet.

That night, it rained heavily. The next morning, I rushed to the window, hoping to see the old man, but he wasn't there. My excitement over playing with the chicken pushed any concern for the old man to the back of my mind. I ran to the coop, only to find the chicken sick and barely able to move. No matter what I did, it refused to "cluck." My mother, seeing how upset I was, returned the chicken to JM the next time she visited. JM, kind as always, returned the penny I had given her, a penny I wanted to give back to the old man—but he was nowhere to be found.

"Maybe he's begging closer to the shelter," my mother suggested when I asked about him. I nodded, though deep down, I felt something was off. That afternoon, on my behest, my mother and I walked through the neighbourhood searching for him. We never found him, and he never returned. I would speculate about what might have happened to him, but all my mother would say was, "I'm sure he's fine somewhere."

A year later, I finally learned the truth—something my mother had known all along from JM. The old man had died that stormy night. They found him soaked and lifeless in a rainwater filled large pothole near the railway tracks. Some said he must have slipped in the downpour and couldn't get back up, that his heart had simply given out in the end. I knew that my mother was trying to shield me from the harsh realities of the world, but I learned my first life lesson early on: Don't give false hopes!

This remains a lesson that frustrates me to this day—the sheer number of people who fail to uphold basic communication in a professional setting. As I matured, I realised that toxic workplace behaviour exists on an entire spectrum.

On one end, there are those who ghost you completely—ignoring your emails because they're unwilling to engage with the content. These individuals leave you hanging without so much as a courtesy reply. On the other end, there are those who outright reject your formal requests without even attempting to understand what you're asking for. You are more likely to be struck by lightning than to receive assistance from these individuals!

Then there's the murky middle ground—the people who already know exactly what they're going to do but still choose to lead you on with false promises. These behaviours commonly manifest as ghost jobs, where a position is technically advertised, but the hiring manager has already decided to fill it internally. Yet, they reassure you that your application is receiving "full consideration." Or your current employer tells you they'll "look into it" after you raise a concern while knowing all along what their final decision will be, wasting your time before revealing an outcome they'd already concluded.

These hollow assurances and delays masked as deliberation don't just waste your time; they erode trust!

Would that penny have saved the old man? Saying "yes" would mean giving a child false hope. Yet, my mother always repeated, "It's the thought that counts!"

As a child, guilt reshaped how I interpreted that phrase. I began to see it as a way to sugarcoat disappointment, to make the giver feel appreciated even when their offering was insufficient, unhelpful, or simply unwanted. Did the contributions I made as a child truly matter, or were they politely dismissed under the guise of gratitude?

If you know something isn't enough, isn't helpful, or simply isn't right, isn't it kinder—more honest—to let the giver know? It might sting in the moment, but it prevents a far deeper disappointment later on.

Three years passed, and gradually, our connection with JM faded. Their farm hit hard times, forcing them to sell the land to a wealthy family and return to their hometown, far from us. After that, it was just our family once again. Fortunately, the last helping hand JM provided chose to stay on. Her name was Rabeya, and she lived in the makeshift room my father built for our domestic help in the open space under the stairwell. Sound familiar? There were two key differences: first, we treated her kindly, and second, a large, bearded man named Hagrid never showed up at our doorstep to tell Rabeya that she was a wizard! Despite that, we cherished her company, even if she wasn't the chosen one!

Life in our household was quiet, almost too simple—a far cry from the bustling world my father once commanded. He had been a successful industrialist, riding high on fortunes that vanished long before I was born, thanks to a series of disastrous investments. By the time I arrived on earth, the echoes of his former life were faint, lingering only in the stories people told about him. He was of average height, with a physique sculpted by disciplined effort—not quite enough to be vain, but enough to show he took pride in himself. His clean-shaven face, all sharp angles and careful grooming, reflected a man who knew exactly how he looked and how to present it. People often remarked on how handsome he was, and I can't help but feel a little flattered when people say I look just like him now, in my early thirties. People used to joke that he never aged, claiming he must've made a deal with the devil. Now they say the same about me—maybe it's a compliment? I suppose I'll take it.

My mother was his partner who witnessed his fall from grace during her tenure as his second wife! She had a face that seemed to invite smiles—soft, round, and fair, catching the light just so. Her large, warm brown eyes held a constant curiosity, or maybe it was kindness—a deep, unshakable belief in the goodness of people that she always seemed to find, no matter where she looked. She never carried bitterness over my father's downfall, at least not outwardly. Instead, there was a quiet strength about her, the kind that made you believe everything could still be alright.

I had a step-sister from my father's previous marriage who was two years older than me. Nida was a burst of energy in human form. Short and full of life, she bounced around like a whirlwind, her wavy hair constantly in motion. Her smile was wide and slightly crooked, accented by a high canine that gave her a playful, mischievous look. She had a way of lighting up any room she entered, her infectious laughter spreading through the air. She was the embodiment of youthful exuberance, never sitting still for too long, and always leaving behind a trail of joy wherever she went. She had just outgrown that phase of obsessively plastering Barbie stickers on every surface that wasn't moving!

I was born around the time my father's bankruptcy was finalised and his assets were being liquidated. That left just me, Nida, and our mother in the house. We had an older gentleman we affectionately called "Chacha" living with us, though we weren't related by blood. He stayed in a small guardhouse beside the main building, a humble space that had been his home for as long as I could remember. Chacha had worked for my father since his youth, back when the businesses were thriving. But when things started to fall apart, so did his prospects. At sixty-five years age, with no other job opportunities and the world not being kind to men his age, Chacha found himself out of work. My father, despite his own financial collapse, insisted on keeping him on as a sort of caretaker for the house, paying him whatever he could scrape together.

Chacha wasn't exactly the most imposing figure. In fact, he was quite the opposite—short and thin, barely taller than young Nida, with a mop of greying hair and a beard that was always just shy of a proper shave. His oversized shirts, which seemed two sizes too big, only added to his diminutive appearance, making him look even shorter than he actually was.

Eventually, my paternal grandmother, whom we lovingly referred to as "*Dadu*," also moved in with us. I was told it was more cost-effective to have her live with us than to cover the costs of her care and care-givers back in our hometown, across the Jamuna River. She was a sweet old lady with a pronounced limp, one that required the aid of a walk-ing stick—though she was far too stubborn to rely on it. Determined to prove she could manage on her own, she often practiced walking from one end of the house to the other, as if to make a point to someone who wasn't even watching. Each slow, deliberate step felt like a quiet rebel-lion against the frailties of age, though none of us had the heart to tell her to take it easy. In her mind, the walking stick was only a suggestion, not a necessity.

Dadu adored me, often saving a little from her personal funds to give to my mother for small treats. Nida had a German Shepherd she named "Sargeant," for reasons known only to her. I always found the name amusing, and you'll see why as the story unfolds. Sargeant stayed with us for almost four years, but eventually succumbed to some dis-ease and the vet had to be him down. Until that time, he had been a cherished part of our family.

As I grew older, I began to appreciate the life we had, especially when I compared it to the struggles of those around us. I learned to show gratitude for good health and access to basic necessities —some-thing the old man on the driveway did not experience in his final days.

We didn't get many visitors, and Nida mentioned that the number had dwindled since my father's businesses failed. It was safe to say he had a lot of fair-weather friends. After all, who would want to be around someone who's grumpy about everything? Occasionally, rel-atives from my father's side would come visit, but my father had an odd habit of avoiding them. He'd hide on the roof until they left. It was strange, but considering his usual grumpiness, it was amusing to watch. Surprisingly, his relatives seemed to understand something that we didn't. They would mostly come to visit *Dadu*, and would bring treats for her which she would later give to me. My mother's side of the family was never welcomed in our home—a situation that didn't change until much later in life.

We always found it entertaining to watch him jump out of whatever he may be doing at the time the moment someone approached the gate or called our telephone to say they were coming. He preferred wearing men's sarongs at home, similar to the villagers nearby. So when he'd hear that someone was on their way, he'd leap up and run to the roof while adjusting his sarong, or "lungi" in Bengali. As I mentioned before, the roof was an unfinished second story—mostly an empty attic room with a rusty metal door that had tower bolts on both sides which separated the roofed and unroofed portions of the second floor. Why both sides? The contractor hired by our landlord made a mistake and accidentally installed one on the wrong side. When it came time to fit the door during our move-in, the contractor, trying to save face, claimed it was intentional, and the door ended up with bolts on both sides.

The unroofed section was bare, with a rough concrete floor and cutouts marking where future rooms were intended. Concrete railings lined the edges, and if you peered over them, you'd see large concrete extensions below, acting as sunshades for the windows of our rooms. Since the building had an older design, these extensions were oversized and often became a hangout spot for the wild monkeys from the nearby trees. Yes, we had wild monkeys and foxes around, and no, they were not cute—they were terrifying and aggressive! For the sake of narration, I will just call the unroofed section "roof" and the roofed section "attic".

The landlord stored unused construction materials in the attic, likely hoping they'd be useful one day—assuming they didn't rust or deteriorate beyond use before that day came. We were convinced the landlord was just renting to us temporarily, until Uttara developed more. Then he'd likely evict us, renovate the place, and lease it to a wealthier family. After all, the area was being marketed as the city's next "rich suburb with culture," whatever that was supposed to mean!

There were several occasions when our landlord would come by to collect the rent, but my father didn't have the money to pay. Instead of facing him, my father would send me to the gate while he dashed upstairs to hide on the roof. I was the scapegoat because the landlord had a soft spot for me—a short, round, cheerful kid—and could never be harsh with me. My father, on the other hand, would have probably been chewed out if he'd dared to face him, and to be fair, the landlord had good reasons!

I was trained to give a standard reply: "Father isn't home today, come back tomorrow." Why I had to keep saying this is beyond me, because I'd end up repeating the same line over and over, even though it was clear no one believed me after the first few times. I vividly remember one time, after I had delivered my Oscar-worthy line for the fifth time, the landlord sighed. As he turned to leave, he said, "Tell your father to stop peeking from over the roof railing. He can't even hide properly!"

It slowly dawned on me why the landlord never bothered to help with any of the repairs around the house. After all, who would go out of their way for a tenant who consistently failed to pay rent on time and resorted to the most childish tactics to avoid confrontation?

Every night, Rabeya had the responsibility of locking the heavy metal door to the deroofed portion of the second floor behind her to keep the blood-sucking tiny predators out! She often complained about the shoddy work the contractor had done—how the bolt and socket never aligned perfectly, making it a struggle to open or close the door.

But that was just one of the many things we had come to accept in our old house, where imperfections seemed to multiply like shadows in the corners.

It was a typical summer night, around 9:00 pm, when my uncle, Colonel Oman, showed up unexpectedly with his family. His car horn blared outside, and as if by instinct, my father's fight-or-flight response kicked in. He bolted toward the stairs leading to the second floor, a routine that had become second nature to him. We had been instructed to take our time unlocking the perimeter gate, a deliberate tactic to give him enough time to escape to the roof and hide from the impending visit.

That night, he grabbed a pack of peanuts from his hidden stash beneath the sofa and hurried up the stairs, adjusting his sarong as he went. One of his many quirky habits was hiding his "treasures"—usually peanuts, biscuits, or other small snacks—under furniture, tucked away from view. These seemingly worthless items were his secret hoard, only discovered in his absence when ants inevitably found their way to the stash first!

As he ran from the impending visit, he ran past the kitchen, where Chacha was helping my mother with dinner preparations. As he approached the stairs, he glanced back at Rabeya's room under the stairwell where he noticed the room door was ajar, but she was nowhere in sight. Ignoring this, he ran upstairs approaching the metal door leading to the roof, only to find it jammed shut. Initially, he thought the bolt was just stuck, as it often was.

"Chacha!" he shouted, his voice carrying as if he were miles away, louder than the sneezes that followed. The scream and sneezes were unrelated but were equally loud. Everyone within a mile radius would have heard him. Unfazed, Chacha casually walked over, and I trailed behind him, curious about the commotion.

"Did you lock the door today? It feels jammed shut," my father continued.

"No, sir. It was Rabeya, as always," Chacha replied.

"So where is she?" My father's brow furrowed with growing worry as he realised the door was locked from the other side. "Why would Rabeya lock herself on the other side?" he murmured.

"Rabeya! What are you doing on the roof so late?" he called out, knocking on the door in an attempt to coax her back. The sound echoed in the stillness of the evening, a rhythmic beat against the metal that felt increasingly ominous.

Just then, I heard hurried footsteps rushed past me and Chacha up the stairs to where my father stood. It was Rabeya, her face flushed and eyes wide with urgency. Panic gripped my father as he turned to her, confusion etched across his face.

Rabeya's expression shifted from concern to horror as she took in my father's look. "Sir, I forgot to lock the door today! I just remembered while I was in the bathroom and heard you call my name!"

The situation was concerning. This wasn't just about a stuck door anymore.

"Who locked the door from the other side?" my father whispered.

Hearing the Colonel's car door open, my father acted on impulse, slamming his shoulder against the door with all his strength. For once, the shoddy misalignment caused the bolt to slip from the socket on the other side. With a creak, the door swung open before him.

Now seems like a good time to tell you that before he became a failed industrialist, he was Lieutenant Oman, a highly regarded officer in the artillery corps and the younger half of the Oman Brothers. Of course, most Bangladeshis couldn't quite pronounce "Lieutenant" correctly and ended up calling him "Left-ten-ant Oman." The brothers had served in the Pakistan Army before the Bangladesh Liberation War of 1971. After the war, they emerged as key figures in their hometown in shaping legislations and maintaining peace within the community. My father's military connections likely aided his rise in the years following the country's independence after his retirement from active service.

He wasn't afraid of what lay beyond the door; rather, he was annoyed that guests were already driving their car up our driveway while Chacha and I were outside opening the gate. My father had planned to spend the evening on the rooftop, perched on his favourite concrete slab. With a handful of peanuts and his gaze fixed on the stars, he would idly fiddle with whatever is in his hands—a habit he had indulged countless times before. The rooftop itself told the story of these quiet moments; scattered peanut shells wedged in the cracks and crevices of his favourite spot bore silent testimony to his nightly retreats.

Downstairs, Colonel Oman, emerged from the car and asked, "Where is your father?" I took a deep breath, ready to deliver my Oscar-worthy line, but before I could speak, we both heard a scream from the roof—not a cry for help, but my father bellowing, "Who's there? Come out of the shadows!" I sighed and replied, "He's on the roof."

"Just like last time!" the Colonel chuckled, but he was cut off as my father called out again to the shadows.

"Does he need help?" the Colonel asked.

"I'll go and ask him," Chacha volunteered, moving toward the stairs. My mother emerged, leading the Colonel and his family into *Dadu's* room while she and Rabeya headed to the kitchen to prepare food for our guests.

Chacha and I walked to close the perimeter gate. I was sure he could manage it alone, but I wanted to feel useful. As we shut the gate, I spotted Sargeant sitting in the walkway beneath the sunshade above my window. This walkway circled the main building and led to his kennel and Chacha's guardhouse out back. I approached Sargeant, noticing him snarl with anger as he glared up at the sunshade. He usually ignored the monkeys, so this was alarming.

Chacha noticed Sargeant's agitation and rushed into the walkway to see what was bothering him. But the darkness concealed whatever had upset the dog.

"Sir! Are you okay?" he yelled to my father on the roof.

"I don't see anything up here. Bring a lantern!" my father called back.

"Right away, sir."

Chacha dashed to his guardhouse, grabbed a lantern, and casually ascended the stairs. I stood with Sargeant, watching the roof light up from below as Chacha reached the top.

"Give it here!" my father shouted, and I assumed he took the lantern from Chacha. The beam of light danced in different directions, suggesting he was searching for something among the shadows.

As a child, I quickly grew bored of watching Sargeant snarl, not grasping the gravity of the situation. I wandered away, and as I passed the stairs to the second floor, it struck me that the door needed closing—otherwise, the mosquitoes would invade. Just as I started up the stairs, I heard my father shout, "There!"

I bolted up the steps, eager to see what the commotion was about, only to catch him charging across the roof, lantern in hand, diving at something—or someone. The lantern hit the ground, flickering as I saw him wrestling a skinny young man wearing a T-shirt and a sarong, the latter folded high up to his hips, presumably to make running easier. Chacha retrieved the lantern while my father roared, "Bloody thief!" because that's exactly what he was—a thief.

Allow me to channel my inner Sherlock Holmes and break down the scene. Picture this like an action movie with the camera guiding you through the details as I piece it all together. If that sounds too much, just bear with me and read on.

The thief had been hiding on the concrete sunshade, right above where Sargeant had been growling earlier. He must have locked the door, planning to wait us out until we fell asleep before sneaking in to steal whatever he could find. What he hadn't anticipated was anyone coming upstairs at that hour. So, when my father began banging on the metal door, the thief panicked. His escape plan was to step over the sunshade and quietly disappear. The problem? Sargeant had sniffed him out and made any silent retreat impossible.

Sargeant was waiting below, ready to pounce if the thief tried to jump down. My father likely heard something but couldn't see the thief, who was crouching in the shadows right beneath him. While my father spoke with Chacha and sent him for the lantern, the thief took his chance to scramble back onto the roof, hoping to flee toward the far side, where he could hop the perimeter wall and vanish into the woods.

Then, my father let out one of his infamous, thunderous sneezes—the kind that could startle anyone, or any thief in this case, within a mile's radius. The sound gave the thief away. In a split second, my father was on him, tackling him with a chokehold.

Burglaries like this were common in Uttara at the time. Some of my school classmates would recount similar stories of thieves from nearby villages breaking into their homes in the middle of the night. These burglars rarely carried weapons, as it would slow them down, and most were too malnourished to put up much of a fight. When they were caught, they were often tied up and handed over to the police in the morning.

This thief was no different. He had no weapon, only the misfortune of trying to rob an army man's house while he was home and on the run from relatives! He attempted to rob a house while a retired Lieutenant, an active Colonel, and "Sergeant" the dog were at home! He must have scoped the place out, knowing my father was often away for days at a time, and wrongly assumed this would be one of those times.

But in the heat of the scuffle, the thief's sarong came loose, unravelling completely. Slipping out of my father's grasp, he bolted for the other side of the roof—bare-bottomed and stark naked—while my father stood there confused and holding the sarong like a victory flag. The thief leaped onto the sunshade, hopped down, and scaled the perimeter fence just as Sargeant lunged at him, narrowly missing his retreating figure. We could hear his wails as he vanished into the woods, probably more terrified than any of us.

Rumour had it that a small crime syndicate in the village coordinated these petty thefts. I couldn't help but wonder how they'd react when this poor fellow returned—empty-handed and bare-cheeked.

My father and Chacha walked past me, exhausted from the scuffle. My father clutched the thief's sarong in his hand, breathing heavily as he made his way down the stairs, his face still flushed with adrenaline. He headed straight to the dining room to wash up. As he passed by *Dadu's* room, the Colonel spotted him through the half-open door. Sitting on one of *Dadu's* sofas, he bellowed my father's name in his deep voice, beckoning him to join them. My father sighed, clearly reluctant, but walked into the room anyway. I would always get nervous too, as I had to be extra mindful of my etiquette and table manners around my father's side of the family—comes with the generational prestige, I suppose!

I trailed behind him, like a curious paparazzo eager to see what would unfold. I took my usual seat—a large, soft couch in the corner that I loved, even though it was much too big for me. My father sat beside his brother, who, to my surprise, didn't acknowledge the commotion that had unfolded upon his arrival. No mention of the thief, no mention of the rooftop. Instead, they launched into a mundane conversation, as though nothing out of the ordinary had happened. They talked for an hour, and I grew bored, eventually heading back to my room to play video games. As I left, I noticed how my father's fingers were still fidgeting with the thief's sarong with a barely noticeable tremor of his head. His gaze had shifted, and he was staring at our guests with a strange intensity. I couldn't tell if he was angry or frustrated, but something in his expression unsettled me. I didn't dare ask him what was wrong—I was terrified of him.

The next morning, the community-appointed security guard rolled up on his bicycle, already aware of the previous night's events. It was suspicious, but we had always suspected he was somehow involved in these petty crimes. Instead of ringing the bell, he knocked on the gate, and Chacha answered. I watched the exchange from my bedroom window. The guard wore a sly grin, extending his hand in a gesture that could only mean one thing: a bribe. My father stepped into the scene, and before I knew it, he snapped. He was seconds away from beating the guard senseless before the man bolted on his bicycle, pedalling as fast as he could.

That was the side of my father that terrified me—his sudden, uncontrollable rage. I had never been on the receiving end of it, but I had seen others face it, like the time with my sister. She had gone to a dress shop in Uttara as a young adolescent and was groped by the shop owner while pretending to assist her in the changing room. She ran home, crying, and told my father. Without hesitation, he marched her back to the shop, made her point out the man, then proceeded to beat him up and destroy his store. He made an example out of him, and from that day on, everyone knew to leave the Lieutenant's daughter alone.

But living with Lieutenant Oman wasn't always about dramatic displays of justice. He enforced military-like discipline in the house, often taking the law into his own hands. The only person exempt from his rules was Nida, his clear favourite. He locked up food in a cabinet and rationed it out, and he only gave us enough money for meals, making sure there was never extra for anything indulgent. Despite his strict rules, my sister defied him when it came to me. After my father had one of his explosive arguments with my mother, she would sneak me treats or toys when he wasn't looking. Occasionally, she'd get caught and scolded, even beaten for other things, but she still looked out for me.

As for me, my father never laid a hand on me. It was as though I didn't exist. He was distant, paying attention to me only when he needed validation as he'd force me onto his lap, demanding that I tell him how much I loved him. I always complied because if I didn't, he would accuse my mother of turning me against him. Otherwise, I was invisible, which wasn't as bad as it might sound. I was his least favourite child, and sometimes I could sense his resentment toward me. I was quiet and calm, and it helped that he was often away, busy trying to salvage his crumbling business ventures.

Life went on. We had our ups and downs, but somehow, we made do. We accepted the hand we were dealt, and for the most part, I had no complaints.

At nine years old, my evenings were primarily spent with my mother, sister, and *Dadu*, as my only true companions. With limited opportunities to socialise outside the house, I had grown socially awkward, but in the presence of these three incredible women, I felt at ease. Sometimes, I could coax Nida into playing video games with me—our favourite was the cult classic *"House of the Dead 2."* I was always Player 2, my role mostly consisting of furiously smashing the space bar whenever something terrifying lunged at us on the screen.

When Nida wasn't around, I'd sit with *Dadu* as she spun tales from her lifetime.

As the months went by, the peaceful routine I had come to cherish started to crumble. My parents started arguing more often, their voices echoing through the house in a stubborn battle of wills. Why? Because they're Asian. Unlike their Western counterparts, who might storm out and vanish into the night, my parents would stay in the same room, even when one of them knew they were dead wrong—ready to go 12 rounds just to prove a point!

Although, I always felt that my father was the one to initiate the fights over his paranoia of things. Nida, who was just a few years older than me, started going to private tutors after school with Chacha, and was not at home as often as she was before. Meanwhile, *Dadu*'s health continued to decline, her frailty becoming more evident with each passing day. Amid it all, I found myself retreating behind tables or sofas, trying to escape the blast radius as my parents clashed.

Sadly, Rabeya had left us by then, something about reasons that my mother said I was too young to fully understand. Her absence left a quiet void in the house. Chacha, who had once been very active around the house, had grown more distant too. Most days, when he was not escorting Nida to her tutors, spent his time in the guardhouse, consumed by his addiction to a tobacco powder called "Gul." He'd taken to it heavily, and it slowed him down—not just physically, but in a way that made him seem older than he actually was. We always knew that he enjoyed gul, but never expected it to consume him entirely.

Our main source of income at the time came from renting out property estates outside the city in an area called Pirojpur that wasn't directly tied to our failing business. These were the last remnants of my father's once-thriving business, which he clung to in a desperate, albeit illegal, attempt to shield them from the looming bankruptcy liquidation. My father would often travel to those estates to manage the rentals, and now started staying away for weeks at a time for reasons undisclosed. He used to drive out in our old Toyota SE Saloon from the early 1990s—his prized possession. My father always had a thing for cars and designer clothes. My sister often recalls how, at the peak of his industrial success, he was one of the first to own an Audi in the country. But when hard times came, the Audi was the first thing he sold. He was so particular about cars that he would even judge homes by the garage and driveways they had. Our own garage was enormous, yet it was rarely occupied because he was always out on the road with his car.

Fast forward a few months: The garage had been empty for a few weeks now because father was away on one of his trips. It was late—far too late for any visitors. The front doorbell rang. The sound jolted all of us. We never had visitors at this hour, especially when my father wasn't home. My mother walked cautiously toward the perimeter gate, asking, "Who is it?" Nida and I stood behind her, just inside the house, peeking out toward the driveway extending beyond the gated perimeter walls. It was dark, and while we could hear voices outside, we couldn't make out who they were.

Suddenly, one of the voices spoke up, calling out my father's name, "Is this Left-ten-ant Oman's house?"

Fear gripped us. My mother's voice trembled as she responded, "Yes... What do you want?"

There was silence on the other side, the tension rising with each passing second. Then, suddenly, a voice broke through—sharp, frantic, and infused with concern. "We found this address in his wallet," the voice spat out. "He's with us... but we don't think he's going to make it. He's bleeding out!"

Chapter 2. Delusion or guilt?

Scepticism vanished the moment my mother rushed out onto the driveway to open the gate. Chacha came out of the guardhouse to respond to the commotion. Standing outside were several villagers with a large trolley, known in Bengali as *thela gari*. The chill in my mother's demeanour was palpable as she urged the villagers to bring the trolley inside. As they pushed it into our yard, I noticed blood dripping onto the ground. Nida instinctively pushed me away, urging me to go to my room. But I could hear the fear in her voice, and as helpless as I felt, I couldn't leave my mother and sister alone in that moment. So I stayed.

On the trolley lay a body, bleeding heavily, trembling, and so bloodied that it was nearly unrecognisable. If the villagers hadn't handed over my father's wallet, we might never have confirmed that it was indeed him on that trolley. That day, I witnessed a side of my mother I had never seen before. She remained remarkably calm, paid the villagers for transporting my father, and rushed inside to call the Military Hospital helpline, urgently requesting an ambulance.

While we waited for the ambulance, my mother asked the villagers what had happened. One of them recounted, "We were sitting at the tea stall on the highway when a long-haul truck suddenly hit the brakes, and we saw the car behind it fly under." Our old Toyota from the 1990s wasn't equipped with airbags, which made the crash even worse.

Another villager chimed in, "We didn't know what to do, but we pulled his body out of the wreckage as best we could. We didn't know if he had any relatives who could pay for hospital fees, so we searched his wallet for an address and brought him here."

In most South Asian countries, admitting a patient to the emergency department of a private hospital often requires a hefty sum of money upfront. There were no public hospitals nearby where my father had crashed, so the villagers believed bringing him home was the best option. During the early 2000s, the military possessed some of the most advanced healthcare facilities in the country. A call for an ambulance was likely the best course of action, and it arrived within fifteen minutes. The villagers who brought him back home saw as the paramedics loaded him in the back of the ambulance, and then left with their trolley once the ambulance left too. My mother left with my father's partially lifeless body in the ambulance, instructing my sister to look after me and *Dadu*. Nida and Chacha closed the perimeter gates behind everyone once they left.

Over the next two weeks, she came in and out of our home to change clothes and bring food to the hospital. She remained by his side in the hospital, caring for him until he made a significant recovery. For the entire month of his recovery, she dedicated herself to being there for him.

During that time, a police officer visited Nida and I during the day.

"I am here regarding Lieutenant Oman's car crashed on the Ashulia Highway. We had the wreckage towed, and we need someone to sign a few documents to either retrieve or permanently dispose of the vehicle," the officer said as we both responded to the doorbell at the perimeter gate.

My sister nodded, agreeing to visit the station with my mother once she returned. Just as the officer turned to leave, she asked, "Have you caught the driver of the truck?"

The officer replied, "We did. He's been handed over to his company officials. From what we gathered at the scene, there's no indication that this was anything but an unfortunate accident. However, we have launched an investigation into the company that hired the driver, as he did not have the appropriate paperwork to be driving such a heavy vehicle."

At the time, I couldn't comprehend why a company would hire someone who didn't meet the required screening criteria. It seemed absurd. But as I grew older, I came to understand that favouritism and nepotism thrive in any economy—whether in Bangladesh or Australia.

If a company wants you, they'll conveniently overlook your shortcomings, just as they'll disregard other applicants who tick every box in their job advertisement.

It took some maturity to grasp this reality. Even in a regulated environment like Australia, meritocracy can falter. If you're skilled enough at something, a company might bypass certain requirements and hand you an opportunity or promotion, even if you don't formally qualify. While it may not apply to road transport businesses, it's relevant to almost every other white-collar industry! And if you believe that audits and regulations would curtail such practices, think again. Take the auditing industry, for instance—many senior auditors are expected to hold a completed Chartered Accountant (CA) certification, yet quite a few serve in their roles with only partial qualifications.

Does this mean they're incompetent? Probably not. Does it mean they're fully qualified? Likely not either. The truth is, certifications hold weight primarily in professions where the stakes are life and death, like healthcare. Elsewhere, the lines blur between formal qualifications, and the ability to deliver results.

Anyway, when we arrived at the police station where the car had been taken the following day with my mother, we could scarcely comprehend how anyone could have survived such a horrific crash. The vehicle was utterly unrecognisable—a twisted mass of metal. The engine was crumpled up against the cracked front windshield, which bore chilling blood spatters. The driver's side door was missing, likely torn off by villagers during the frantic rescue attempt.

What probably saved his life was the fact that the steering wheel hadn't completely caved in, leaving just enough space to prevent his lungs from being crushed. After a long, painful silence, we made the decision to have my father's beloved car that's been with us for years disposed of.

If you think this is the beginning of a vigilant child's crime scene investigation arc, you're reading the wrong story. I was just a scared young kid, recently enrolled in Taekwondo by my mother at the new studio that had opened next door. She didn't sign me up to help me defend myself; she was worried that I was putting on too much weight and simply wanted me to get into shape and adopt a more active lifestyle.

Let's be real: you can't fight crime as a caped crusader at night with only white belt-level Taekwondo skills! Just kidding—Taekwondo looks impressive in demonstrations, but in a real fight, you need your hands more than your feet.

To our surprise, my father made a remarkable recovery in just two months, and the surgeons achieved impressive results in reconstructing his face. Aside from a few long scars along his jawline, which softened its once-prominent definition and blurred the boundary between his neck and chin, the outcome was exceptional. There were also faint scars behind his ears that pulled the skin slightly, likely from the incision sites, and a subtle asymmetry in his lip on one side. Regardless, the outcome was exceptional.

You'd think that after everything my mother did for him, my father would have changed—that he would be kinder, that they would stop fighting. But within months of him recovering, the fights resumed, this time worse than it was before.

One weekend morning, I was playing with a pink toy fighter jet, gripping its wheel as I ran around the house. As I flew it into the dining room, I suddenly heard my father scream and curse at my mother. Startled, I dropped the toy and hid under the dining table. It was large and made of dark wood, casting deep shadows under the light above, allowing me to stay concealed in my dark clothing.

I watched as my mother stormed into her room as my father followed. He was shouting while my mother kept ignoring him. My mother said something that I could not comprehend from where I was. The argument escalated suddenly and quickly. I rushed to the doorway, and before I could react, I saw him punch my mother in the stomach. Frozen, I stood there as he unbuckled his belt and began beating her with it, pushing her onto the bed as she cried for help. I felt utterly powerless. He noticed me standing in the doorway and slammed the door shut in my face before continuing his attack. I could still hear her cries from the other side, but I didn't know what to do.

In shock, I stumbled outside to the driveway and sat down, struggling to process what had just happened. My chest tightened, and I could suddenly hear the pounding of my own heart—something I'd never noticed before. I was sweating profusely, and I started having a headache. Was this a panic attack?

I watched as my father hurried to the small storage room he called home. He grabbed his travel bag and, with swift, practiced movements, locked the door using an old, rusted padlock—one with a distinct red vertical stripe running down one side. Without a word, he left, disappearing for a month. From that day forward, he began locking the room with that same antique padlock whenever he wasn't home, as if guarding some secret hidden behind its weathered door.

When I recovered and finally mustered the courage to return to the room, I found her lying there, bruised, swollen, unable to move. I crawled onto the bed and placed my hand on her shoulder, at which point she weakly wrapped an arm around me before passing out from the pain. I stayed with her for the next several hours until she regained consciousness.

Do I know exactly why that happened? No. Does it make me angry? Absolutely. Could I have done anything about it? No. Did I feel utterly helpless? Yes. But I believe that was when my mother began planning her escape. Like a chess game, she had to strategise carefully. She couldn't just walk out—she had no job to support us and was entirely dependent on my father's income. And leaving me behind with him? That was never an option. She knew how terrified I was of him.

I once asked my mother, "He is always so terrible to you. He is violent. Why did you go above and beyond to help him? Did you never think he got what he deserved?" She silenced me with a look, then replied: "If someone needs your help and you are able to offer it, you give it. We don't leave a person when they are in need because we reap what we sow." This would later become my second life lesson: "Karma is a b*tch!"

The violence at home escalated. Sometimes, the arguments between my parents became so intense that Nida would take me to her room, covering my ears, trying to shield me from the chaos. My mother was reaching her breaking point, ready to leave despite not finding a job, when *Dadu* collapsed, with multiple organs failing, and she could no longer recognise anyone.

I can already hear my Western readers chiming in, "So what? She's not *your* mum—get out while you still can, love! Ta!" And honestly, my mother's family was on the same page, sharing the same sentiment. Despite everyone advising her to leave, my mother chose to stay and care for *Dadu*. She pleaded with my father to hire help to which he agreed, obviously. But with his cash running low and JM gone, he didn't know who else to turn to. Nowhere else to turn, he reached out to our questionable community-appointed security guard, who gladly gave him the contact of a man named Ranjan Marya, known for supplying help. He got in touch with Ranjan and paid for a few village women from rural Bangladesh to serve as makeshift nurses, along with a professional nurse who would visit once a week. But the village women, though cost-effective, weren't trained caregivers, and *Dadu's* condition worsened.

At this point, my mother stopped searching for jobs. She felt her duty was to care for *Dadu*, and for the next year, that's exactly what she did. It wasn't easy. The makeshift nurses were poorly equipped to handle *Dadu's* care, and my paternal relatives started visiting more frequently, commenting constantly about *Dadu's* gold and savings. They insisted my mother safeguard the wealth, though she showed no interest in material possessions. In fact, she had sold all the jewellery she received during her wedding to help pay the bills when my father couldn't afford anything for a few years.

Watching these relatives, more preoccupied with family politics than *Dadu*'s well-being, pained my mother deeply. As a child, I couldn't grasp the full weight of what was unfolding, but I could sense the strain in every interaction. I remember my mother pleading with Colonel Oman, often about my father's behaviour. He would dismissively say, "I don't want to get involved. Obik's personal affairs should be handled by family." Every time, my mother would break down, her voice trembling with frustration as she cried, "Stop enabling him!"

The only thing I knew was that my mother stayed in that house to care for *Dadu*. Even the maids picked up on the household's tension. They saw how my father stopped respecting my mother and occasionally beat her in front of them. The girls stopped taking my mother seriously, believing that she had no real authority since my father didn't respect her. This dynamic persisted for months. My mother was trapped, not by fear, but by a sense of duty—her care for *Dadu* came first.

By the late 2000s, *Dadu* had lost all sense of reality. She no longer recognised any of us. In her mind, I was my father as a young man training for the army, and she often thought she was back in her village, reliving the early years of her marriage. She kept reliving her days of being a young adult, talking about how childhood Polio had left her weak, and she would talk endlessly about how the illness had strained her relationship with her in-laws. Sometimes I would sit with her, listening to her stories as night fell, but schoolwork and the daily chores kept me busy most nights. My mother, on the other hand, never left her side. The village girls who had been hired to help stopped showing up to work. They had secluded themselves to the small lodging in the garage that my father built for them—no longer needed now that we didn't have a car. But as Uttara developed further with wealthier families moving in, one by one, the girls left for better job prospects and higher pay, until only two remained, Anna and Riba. Anna and Riba were both petite, but that was where the similarities ended. Anna, in her mid-twenties, bore the marks of a hard life—her face weathered by struggles that had aged her beyond her years. Riba, on the other hand, claimed to be eighteen but appeared much younger, with a soft, round face that contrasted sharply with her cold, detached gaze. While Anna's warmth was evident in her every movement, Riba's presence felt distant, almost unsettling.

Even as a child, it was easy for me to tell them apart. Anna's care for *Dadu* was tender, her hands steady and her demeanour comforting. Riba, though, with her pale complexion and unblinking eyes, seemed like a shadow—there, but not really present.

It was September. My father had been away for several weeks, as usual. I remember it was a humid evening, with a smell of damp earth in the air, the kind that warns of an approaching storm. The wind whistled through the cracks in the windows of our old house, which by then had fallen into a state of neglect. The house itself mirrored the condition of our family—crumbling, worn down by years of unresolved tension and unspoken pain.

Nida was in her room, working on school assignments. Meanwhile, I was in my room. I shared my room with my mother, and we had two beds. My bed was bigger than hers because I liked rolling around in my sleep and often fell over. Her bed was positioned next to the window—the same window where, as a child, I used to watch the old homeless man who sat on our driveway.

I will go off topic now, but I assure you that it is relevant to the story...somewhat!

I had a cousin, the Colonel's only son, who lived in the UK. His visits to Bangladesh were rare, but one of them was for a particularly memorable occasion—to marry one of the kindest and sweetest people I had ever met. Their marriage was arranged—a concept that might seem foreign to my Western readers. In this tradition, both families come together to weigh the pros and cons of the union, much like medieval noblemen negotiating marriages of convenience. The reasoning behind it is that love can lead us to make impulsive decisions, while families tend to approach such matters with a more rational mindset. However, the downside is that you can never truly know how your partner will turn out.

While I don't advocate for either love or arranged marriages, I can confidently say that my sister-in-law's choice worked out well—at least for me! They frequently convinced my cousin to buy me gaming consoles, starting with the PlayStation 1 and later the PlayStation 2. Most recently, they even gifted me the laptop I used for university. But the one purchase my cousin probably regretted was a video camera I used to film my sister-in-law's tearful reaction when her parents entered the room and informed her she would have to marry the guy sitting on the couch.

You might wonder why I was even present for that conversation. The truth is, no one noticed I was there, silently recording the entire exchange as tears streamed down her face as she expressed her disapproval. It wasn't until Nida realised I was missing that she burst into the room and yanked me away.

My cousin was concerned about what I might do with the footage. So, when I excitedly shared the footage with him, he promised to take the tapes back to the UK, edit them into a video, and send it back to me. I eagerly agreed, but I never saw that video again. I later realised he likely destroyed it—for good reason!

Why is that relevant to this story? That evening, I was playing video games on a PlayStation 2 my sister-in-law had recently sent from the UK. The TV was perched on a small stand next to my mother's bed where I sat playing, the soft glow of the screen offering some comfort against the howling wind outside. I was fully engrossed in the game when I heard something—a distinct crunching sound, like dry leaves being stepped on, just outside my window. Okay, now that I think about it, my cousin's story wasn't probably all that relevant here!

But now, this is where the rest of the layout of our Uttara house becomes important.

The main building had three bedrooms, one occupied by my mother and I, one for Nida, and one for *Dadu*. My father converted a storeroom without windows into his temporary lodging during the limited time he spent with us. He didn't have a bed; instead, he would sleep on the carpeted floor, which I assumed was to ease his back pain. Still, I always found it strange that he chose to sleep there of all places and it made me wonder why he preferred the confines of a storeroom. There was a closed garage on one side that once served to house my father's Toyota, which was later transformed into a makeshift bunk-style lodge for the helping hands looking after *Dadu*. The room at the base of the stairwell remained vacant since Rabeya left. The house was built in such a way that a narrow walkway wrapped around the entire building, separating the house walls from the high perimeter walls that surrounded our property. The walkway allowed access to the backyard, where we had a water pump and holding tank that supplied water to the house. The design was old and practical, but it wasn't aesthetically pleasing. In fact, it felt more like a pathway that led to nowhere—uninviting and eerie, especially at night.

Our room and *Dadu's* room were connected by a common balcony that faced this walkway, which took a sharp elbow turn near the balcony and wrapped around both rooms. From there, it circled around the rest of the house, eventually leading to the kitchen window on the opposite side. The walkway was long and spacious, with several jackfruit and lemon trees that grew close to the walls, their dense foliage casting shadows and making it difficult to see in certain places.

From my window, I could only see part of the driveway, but I knew the rest of the walkway well. It had once been home to my sister's German Shepherd, who was now buried next to his kennel. The dog's kennel remained in the back, built slightly larger than necessary. Since Sargeant's passing, the paint on the doghouse had worn away, leaving it looking like a rusted, dilapidated structure. Only two lights lined the entire perimeter, leaving most of the walkway in darkness, adding to the sense of disrepair and abandonment that now characterised our home.

The sound of crunching leaves persisted, growing louder, as if someone were slowly making their way around the house. My heart raced, and I paused the game, straining to listen. The wind howled through the cracks in the walls, blurring the line between the storm's natural rumble and the footsteps outside. I glanced at my mother, who was fast asleep on my bed, exhausted from caring for *Dadu*.

A few years ago, I would have dismissed this noise as nothing more than Sargeant, our German Shepherd, patrolling the perimeter. But now, we don't have a dog remember? as a twelve-year-old who spent countless hours immersed in investigative video games, curiosity urged me to explore.

At that time, political unrest was rampant, leading to severe budget cuts. Electricity, a basic necessity, was often sacrificed. You'd think it would be a priority, but this was a country where leaders debated whether to ban pornography from the internet over more important matters of national interest, so why wouldn't they consider load shedding a cost-saving measure? We experienced power outages five to six times a day, each lasting an hour. Just as I stepped out of my room, the electricity went out—"*great, there goes my game save,*" I thought.

I rushed back to grab a flashlight. Venturing into our shared balcony, the one we used with *Dadu*, I swept the beam outside but saw nothing. *Dadu* heard my footsteps and, in her delusion, called out to me using my father's name. I approached her in the darkness. She was trembling, repeating that she was scared and pleading for me not to leave her side. As I watched her pant, it struck me that she was likely experiencing an anxiety attack. She had been diagnosed with late-stage dementia, and we were warned that she could often get delusional and stuck in her past. But tonight felt different—unnatural.

"I'll be right back," I promised, and I ran to my mother, waking her gently. "*Dadu* needs help; she's restless." My mother immediately got up and went to see her. True to my words, *Dadu* was shivering uncontrollably and running a fever. My mother asked me to rush to the garage to get her appointed carers, who could help lift *Dadu*—completely bedridden by that point. My mother feared *Dadu* might develop bedsores if the fever broke and she began to sweat on the oilcloth spread beneath her.

I dashed to the garage and opened the door, finding Anna asleep, but Riba was missing. Not thinking much of it, I woke Anna and had her follow me to *Dadu*'s room, where the old woman was shivering violently.

"Where's Riba?" Anna wondered aloud as she followed me inside.

Amidst her fever, *Dadu* began to recoil, her voice rising in frantic urgency as she repeated, "They are after my gold; they're planning to kill me! They're planning to kill me!" Her words were heavy with fear. It felt disturbingly lucid as she pointed toward the window, where white curtains filtered in the moonlight, casting shadows of swaying tree branches against the wall. Her eyes were wide with terror. "I heard them; they're planning to kill me!"

Chapter 3. Passed away

If I wanted to build tension and be dramatic about the turn of events, I might have said something like this: The clouds finally broke, and the storm poured down as I slowly approached the curtains. *Dadu* screamed and cried as I hesitated, pulling the curtains away, unaware of the horrors that awaited me. With a sudden yank, I flung them open, and what I saw shocked me to my core!

But that's not what happened at all. The wind was howling, but it hadn't rained all night—a false alarm! I dashed to the curtains and pulled them aside, but *Dadu* was completely unfazed, lost in her own world as she began reminiscing about her childhood. Meanwhile, my mother and Anna were more concerned about her bedsores.

When I yanked the curtains, I discovered that one of the curtain rollers was stuck on the rail, preventing them from opening fully. I managed to peek through the small opening I'd created, but what I found was nothing—just the wind rattling the leaves and darkness stretching as far as my eyes could see. I couldn't help but think, "I am an idiot!"

The only concerning aspect of the entire situation was that Riba was still missing. She hadn't returned by morning, and when we went to check, we discovered she had left with her bags. This wasn't entirely irregular; most of the girls moved on without informing us after some time, with Anna being the lone exception. She remained by *Dadu*'s side until the very end.

The only outsider who was more consistently present in our lives than Anna was our landlord—a man who, let's face it, was barely keeping it together. He was desperately trying to scrape together enough money to renovate the crumbling house we lived in and replace us with a wealthier tenant. My father's habit of chronically paying the rent late only added to his misery. Who could have seen that coming?

This morning wasn't great. *Dadu*'s fever didn't break like it had before. By noon, my mother and Anna decided to take her to Minister Kuddus Memorial Hospital in Uttara, or "Kuddus Memorial" as the locals called it. If the name sounds absurd, it's because our politics often is. Minister Kuddus was very much alive, despite the "Memorial" part, which might confuse you. He never went to school, and that could be a reason for the peculiar name. When politicians take office, one of their first moves is to rename everything—even things that don't need renaming—just to satisfy their own inflated egos. Is it a complete waste of taxpayer money? Absolutely.

Mother's initial plan was a quick check-up, with *Dadu* returning home before dinner. But once at the hospital, the doctors advised that her condition had deteriorated significantly since the last nurse visit. They suggested keeping her admitted for tests. By the afternoon, her health worsened, and my mother was told to prepare for a stay in the ICU—at least five more days of hospitalization.

My mother and Anna came home to pack for the long stay. I watched as they gathered clothes from *Dadu*'s closet and packed her meds and hygiene supplies. Before leaving, my mother made sure the oilcloth on *Dadu*'s bed didn't dampen the quilt, layering a pillow between the oilcloth and the quilt. I looked at the arrangement and joked, "It looks like someone's sleeping under the quilt." My mother chuckled, but it was clear she was too worried about *Dadu* to fully appreciate my low-quality joke.

She packed some food for herself and Anna, announcing they'd be spending the night at the hospital. With a sigh, she mentioned how much she wished Chacha could have been around to look after us, but he was off at the Pirojpur property with my father. Probably running errands while my father tried to negotiate a lease agreement with a pharmaceutical company—a deal that might finally pull him out of bankruptcy.

So, it was just Nida and me again—just like old times. The only difference was that she now had lots of friends, while I remained the socially awkward kid with none. At least I had my video games, as long as there wasn't another bout of load shedding. Only Nida had access to the internet—through broadband, no less!—but no WiFi yet. It had taken her ages to convince our father that our ancient dial-up wasn't cutting it, and that 8kbps broadband was the future! For context, in 2024, broadband speeds in Australia average over 800,000kbps! What did we use our smouldering fast connection for? MSN Messenger, of course! I'll spare my younger readers the pain of explaining MSN Messenger in detail. I had an account on my sister's computer, but barely used it... because, well, I had no friends outside of the ones I grew up with at school.

Anyway, I digress. My mother and Anna left with supplies, and Nida closed the perimeter gates behind them. I jokingly mentioned hearing leaves crunching out back, and my mind wandered to dramatic scenarios. Nida laughed, suggesting it was probably Sargeant's ghost. That's when I learned Sargeant had passed away. Shame! I still felt inclined to check out back, just to put my mind at ease, but for some reason, I hesitated. As I passed the entrance to the perimeter walkway, I felt that eerie sensation again—like something had moved the leaves. I shrugged it off as my imagination and walked away, but after a few steps, I retraced my path and stared again at the long, leaf-covered walkway. It had been ages since anyone cleaned it.

I decided to investigate anyway and thought it would be fun to make a documentary of my "investigation." I rushed back to my room and grabbed the video camera my cousin had sent me. It was one of those models with the cassette slots that opened from the bottom, no SD card support—just a single overwritable magnetic cassette tape. The tapes were proprietary, hard to find, and the camcorder itself had gone out of style quickly, replaced by newer models with USB support. For most, it wasn't worth much, but for me, it held sentimental value as a gift from a loved one, making it priceless in its own way. I opened the LCD screen and turned the camera on, ready to film my grand return to the walkway after two years. Honestly, even I had forgotten what the backyard looked like. All I remembered was the lemon tree I'd planted, which used to yield four lemons a season that I sold to *Dadu* for 100 taka. For reference, lemons weren't expensive in the market, but your grandson's lemons? Priceless.

It felt like an eternity walking to the first bend in the path. The walkway wrapped around the house, leading to the far side where Sargeant's kennel used to be. The lemon tree stood near the first bend, close to our shared balcony. Balancing the camera while walking and trying to focus on the screen was no easy feat. I suddenly realised I hadn't pressed record. I hit the red button, only to be greeted with the message: *Cassette not found*. I remembered then that my cousin had taken the only cassette I had, and despite my efforts, I never found a replacement in Bangladesh for that model. "*So much for my horror documentary!*" I thought.

Still, I kept the camera rolling for the fun of it, checking the screen occasionally to see if it looked remotely as eerie as *The Blair Witch Project*—yes, I'm that old! I made it to the bend and spotted my lemon tree, which was now dying from lack of care. I glanced up at our balcony, and through *Dadu's* door, I saw something odd. "*Dadu's* at the hospital—who's on *Dadu's* bed?" I zoomed in, only to realise it was the pillow my mother had put under the quilt. I laughed at myself, remembering my own joke from earlier.

I continued walking towards the second bend, remembering how there used to be monkeys in this area. But since the whole neighbourhood had developed, they had disappeared, along with most of the trees. The once beaten paths had transformed into proper asphalt roads. "*Uttara has come a long way,*" I thought to myself.

I walked up to *Dadu's* room window. The windowsill was chipped in one corner, and the paint had begun to fade. One of the trees had grown just enough to let a tiny branch brush against the window, rattling with the wind. "Maybe that's what *Dadu* heard last night," I mused.

As I passed the second bend and approached the third, I realised this was where the water pump and Sargeant's old kennel were. It was also a dead end, and I thought, "*It's going to be a long walk back if I go all the way around.*" But curiosity got the better of me, and I still wanted to see what Sargeant's "ghost" might look like. In my mind, I was probably recreating a scene from Stephen King's *Pet Sematary*, imagining Sargeant back in his kennel out behind the house, waiting for me. The thought sent a chill down my spine, but I couldn't help pushing forward.

We barely had any lights installed there—just one that overlooked Sargeant's kennel. The third bend was also near the kitchen window, and I remembered how Sargeant would often stand on his hind legs, paws pressed against the window, begging for food. Just before I turned the corner, I heard a shrill, familiar voice call my name: "Yaad!"

It wasn't a soft, creepy ghost voice. It was annoyed, sharp, and very human. I knew who it was. I turned around, and sure enough, there was Nida on the shared balcony.

"What are you doing down there?" she asked.

"Nothing, just checking on my lemon tree," I replied, trying to sound casual.

"Well, hurry up. Food's ready, and I'm starving."

I nodded and, deciding I wasn't quite ready for any ghostly encounters, ran back, passing the second and first bends without stepping foot onto the third.

After dinner, my sister told me she was going to her room and offered, with a hint of teasing, that I could join her if I was too scared to sleep alone. Offended, but hiding my actual nerves, I waved her off. "I'm fine, I don't need you," I said, even though I kind of did. I wasn't used to sleeping in an empty room without my mother. She rolled her eyes and went to her room.

I always prided myself on being the more responsible sibling, so I remembered that at sunset, mosquitoes were a big issue, and I should close all the doors to keep them out. At around 6:00 pm., I rushed upstairs to the second floor. Before closing the large metal door—now corroded from years of neglect—I decided to step out onto the roof for old time's sake.

The cool air hit my face as I leaned against the concrete railing, looking out over the streets and houses. I remembered how, when I was younger, my mother would rub oil on my skin, give me a lolly, and send me up to the roof to bask in the sun until I'd finished the candy. Then I'd come back downstairs. But what my twelve-year-old self was reminiscing about up there on that roof that day... that's beyond me.

And you might ask, "Wait, Yaad, how do you remember that day so well?"

Well, keep reading and you'll find out!

The Maghrib Azan echoed from a nearby mosque, filling the air with its solemn call. Beyond signalling time for prayer, it also meant that dusk had arrived. I hurried back inside, sliding the tower bolt into place. After that roof fiasco with the thief, my father had insisted on calling the contractor to remove the bolt on the outside. He also installed a few extra lights in the backyard, though he never got around to connecting them to the main power board. Eventually, he lost interest, reasoning, "Lights won't keep danger out. We just need to be vigilant and lock everything up!"

For me, the real threat was mosquitoes. If we didn't close every window and door tightly, they'd swarm the house, making it impossible to stay indoors comfortably. Why is that relevant? Well, I knew for sure that I had securely closed everything.

Just like last night, at around 9:00 pm the air was humid, carrying the earthy scent that signals an approaching storm. The wind was fierce, repeatedly slamming the metal door to the roof. The sound crept in under the balcony door as I sat in my room, engrossed in *Bullworth Academy*. It was the British version of Rockstar Games' hit *Bully*, where you played as a school troublemaker, making friends and completing mischievous missions. I'm not saying I was living vicariously through a video game because I lacked a social life...but, I wasn't *not* doing that either.

Of course, that was until the fourth round of load shedding hit. "Perfect, just one more left for the night," I muttered, dropping the controller onto the bed. I wandered over to my study table, where the video camera sat. I picked it up, fiddling with it absentmindedly before setting it back down. Maybe it was being alone in such a big room, but I couldn't shake the feeling that I was being watched. I know, cliché, but when you feel it, you feel it.

I glanced at the curtains covering my window. Like *Dadu*'s, they only closed so far before the rollers jammed. Unlike hers, though, mine always got stuck while closing, leaving a small gap between them. When the electricity was on, the room was bright, making the darkness outside impenetrable. But now, with the load shedding, the faint light outside allowed me to see a little through the gap, and every small sound was amplified in the silence. It was odd because I could also hear the buzzing of mosquitoes, and they were coming from inside the room.

That's when I heard it—leaves crunching again. I stepped closer to the window, squinting into the darkness, hoping to spot whatever was causing the noise. But there was nothing. Then, I heard more crunching, this time by the lemon tree. If I'm honest, I was already terrified, and there was no way I was stepping out onto the balcony to investigate. Looking back, I think that was the smarter choice.

I grabbed my flashlight—since I didn't own a phone back then—turned it on, and headed toward Nida's room. Our kitchen didn't have a door; a quirk of the landlord who never bothered installing one after we moved in. As I passed through the kitchen, I noticed something odd. I glanced over with my flashlight, and I froze in place. One of the kitchen windows was wide open.

It explained how the mosquitoes had gotten in, but not how the window had opened in the first place. Still, I wasn't too concerned. All our windows had metal railings for security, and although they opened outward, I could squeeze my hand between the bars to pull it shut. So, I reached out, gripped the lever, and began to close it. As I did, the sound of crunching leaves echoed again—this time, much closer, near Sargeant's kennel just a few feet away.

I tried to dismiss it, telling myself, *"It's just my mind playing tricks."* Quickly, I locked the window and rushed out of the kitchen, continuing on my way to my sister's room. Her room was on the other side of the house, which meant crossing the stairs to the second floor. As I passed, the wind howled louder, slamming the metal door on the roof.

I ignored everything else and rushed to Nida's room. She was lounging on her bed, engrossed in a Sidney Sheldon novel, using a torch she had balanced under her chin to read in the dim light. A true bookworm, she always had her nose in a book. Her collection was so large that after filling the shelves in her room, she took over the ones in ours, and still, many of her books ended up in a metal trunk now stashed in the garage. She was the type of person who got so lost in the narrative that she became completely unaware of her surroundings when reading.

Playfully, I flashed the light in her eyes. She groaned, telling me to knock it off. I jumped onto her bed, instantly feeling a sense of relief. Her window faced the walkway outside, where there were no dry leaves like those near my room, which had fuelled my paranoia.

While she read her book, I amused myself by making shadow puppets on the wall with my flashlight. It was oddly comforting, and before I knew it, I drifted off to sleep—without brushing my teeth. Sorry, future me.

I remember dozing off with the lights out because of load shedding. At around 2:00 am., I woke up briefly. My eyes adjusted to the lights now blazing around the house. I realised we'd left all the lights on. Nida was fast asleep beside me. I tried to wake her, but she brushed me off.

Feeling an urgent need to turn everything off, I got out of bed, suddenly forgetting all the fear and paranoia that had haunted me earlier. A well-lit room can do that to you. I made my way out, switching off lights as I went. But then I paused—something didn't feel right. The lights in the corridor outside my room and *Dadu's* were already off. *"Did I turn them off earlier?"* I wondered. It didn't make sense, but I shrugged it off. *"Less work for me,"* I thought.

I returned to my room, noticing that my PlayStation was on standby. I turned it off, put the controllers away, and headed to the bathroom to brush my teeth. As I moved through the house, I felt like something was missing, but I couldn't figure out what. I looked left and right, but everything seemed normal, so I chalked it up to exhaustion and brushed it off.

After brushing my teeth, I went back to my room. As much as I liked being in my sister's room, I needed my own space to sleep—I tend to move around a lot. I lay down, feeling myself slowly drifting back to sleep, when suddenly, I heard a metallic thud.

I froze, listening. It sounded like a metal bar dropping from some height. I scanned the room, but nothing seemed out of place. Then, I heard faint voices—one coming from the shared balcony, the other from the corridor.

I was alarmed. We weren't alone in the house.

How could I warn Nida? I didn't have a phone, and I couldn't just call for help. I was almost certain that the noise came from *Dadu's* room, as the sound felt too distant to be from the other side of the perimeter walls but too close to be anywhere else. I sat on my bed, paralysed with fear.

The only thing I could muster the courage to do was lock the doors leading to the balcony and the dining room corridor. I prayed silently, hoping this would all just pass. I lay back in bed, listening to the faint sound of footsteps—barefoot, soft—pacing around the balcony and dining room. The sound slowly faded toward *Dadu*'s room, and I heard the door close behind them.

In that moment of terror, I somehow drifted off to sleep, too afraid to move. I should've run to Nida, but the fear had paralysed me. Even as I heard the indistinct voices fade away, I stayed frozen in bed, until I started hearing my heart pound in my chest again. The palpitations started until sleep finally overtook me.

I woke up the next morning, drenched in sweat. At first, I chalked it all up to a horrible nightmare, a product of spending the night alone in my room. A wave of relief washed over me, but only for a moment. Then I glanced at my study table and realised—the video camera was gone!

A sinking feeling hit me hard. Something had happened last night. My heart raced as I slowly opened my door, peeked down the corridor, and then bolted to Nida's room. She was still asleep, thankfully. I grabbed her phone and called my mother. She rushed home as fast as she could.

Even as I waited, I wasn't sure if I'd imagined the whole thing. After all, I was only twelve years old, and my mother had always said I had an overactive imagination. But when she arrived, she went straight for *Dadu*'s room. She tried to open the door, but it was locked from the inside. The eerie silence behind the door sent chills down my spine. She immediately called the police and my father.

When they arrived, the police broke down the door, and what we saw confirmed my worst fears—*Dadu*'s room had been completely ransacked. All her belongings were scattered across the floor, and her jewellery box had been broken into.

A second group of police officers made their way around the back, following the muddy prints from *Dadu*'s window toward the third bend near the water pump. There, they found a section of the metal railing of *Dadu*'s window cut clean through, with a trail of clothes and personal items leading away. They followed the trail and discovered a small break in the wall near the water pump. It looked like whoever had broken in used it as a foothold to scale the perimeter walls, carrying a heavy sack of stolen goods. The officers grew suspicious—it was too much work for just one night. This had likely been in the making for three or four nights.

Back at *Dadu*'s window, they found multiple footprints in the mud. Some were fresh, others had hardened, meaning *Dadu* hadn't been imagining things. In her confused state, she really had heard someone on the other side of her window. One officer found another set of fresh prints in the passageway outside my own window—the spot where I'd been last night playing on my Playstation. The officer noted that the footprints were too small to be a man's, likely belonging to a child or a woman. They also suggested that the break-in seemed too coordinated, as if someone familiar with the house had provided inside information. At that point, all we could do was speculate. Without concrete evidence, I don't want to cast accusations in what I write here.

The disappearance of the camera left me uneasy. Had the intruders taken it, mistaking it for something valuable? Or had someone seen me with it, thinking they were caught on film? To this day, I can only guess. But what truly haunts me is the thought of what might have happened if I hadn't fallen asleep in Nida's room that night when the lights went out. Imagine lying in bed, knowing you're alone in the house, only to hear the door creak open and catch a glimpse of an unfamiliar figure peeking in from the other side!

But the worst part of all? There was a huge gash in the quilt on *Dadu*'s bed, sliced through with a sharp blade. It tore deep into the pillow that my mother had placed there before she left. The thought terrified me—someone had thought there was a person under that quilt. *Dadu* had heard someone say they would kill her and take all her gold.

It wasn't just her imagination after all.

A few days later, *Dadu* passed away in the hospital, blissfully unaware of the horrors that could have awaited her. Had she not developed a fever the night before and been rushed to the hospital, things might have been tragically different.

Chapter 4. Uprooted

It was early morning. My mother and Anna bathed *Dadu*'s body as a religious custom before performing their last prayer for her, while the Colonel sat in *Dadu*'s room trying to console his younger brother. My father was crying, howling even, and the sound carried all the way to the roof where I stood, through the open window under me. Though he had been in denial at the hospital, he finally accepted what had happened once *Dadu*'s body was brought home for the final religious rites.

I overheard the Colonel say, "I have to decide where to bury her." My father didn't respond. The Colonel repeated, "We should bury her back in Naogaon." Naogaon was our hometown, across the Jamuna River, where my father grew up, surrounded by vast empty land. He spent years serving in the newly formed Bangladesh Army before retiring from active service while still in his thirties. The circumstances of his early retirement were always unclear, something only *Dadu* and my uncle fully understood.

My uncle, who had also served in the military, stayed in the service and eventually became a Colonel, earning respect and receiving land for his service. Meanwhile, my father transitioned into becoming an industrialist, rising in influence before facing financial decline long before his brother even considered retirement. Despite everything, he had recently begun to recover, having sold some of the uncontested land he owned in Pirojpur to a local pharmaceutical company that somehow pulled him out of bankruptcy. In trying to save his failing business, he had been away during *Dadu*'s final days, and I think that weighed heavily on him.

Soon, the rest of the family arrived, and our large driveway filled with cars, stretching down the newly paved road. Family from near and far gathered to pay their final respects to *Dadu*. She had been the glue holding the family together, and many of them likely tolerated my father's eccentricities and temper because of her.

I stood on the roof with Nida, watching as more cars pulled up. Families stepped out and entered through our wide-open gates as my mother guided them inside to *Dadu's* room. At the second bend of the walkway, we noticed a contractor welding additional rebars onto *Dadu's* window for added security.

Then, I saw a police car arrive.

"Who in our family is a police officer?" I asked my sister, confused.

"No one," she replied. Two officers got out and walked straight into the house, passing *Dadu's* body. Later, my mother explained that they had come to inform us the case wasn't classified as a murder, only a robbery, which meant it ranked lower on their priority list. As with most places, felonies without strong evidence tend to fall by the wayside, especially when forensic teams aren't involved from the outset. The cost of conducting forensic investigations is high, and our local authorities simply didn't have the resources. As a result, the case was never solved.

The police left within minutes, and shortly after, a small freezer truck pulled up.

"Who is it now?" I asked.

Nida replied, "Ice, for the journey." I didn't understand. She explained, "They're probably taking *Dadu's* body back to Naogaon, and the ice will keep it from decomposing in the heat during the journey." Embalming isn't a common practice in our culture, so bodies are typically buried within a day. For long journeys, placing the body on ice inside a freezer truck is the most practical and affordable option, a practice still used today.

Half an hour went by.

"We should head back downstairs," my sister said, noticing some of our cousins, who were around our age, getting out of one of the cars.

I agreed and we came downstairs. I saw my father on his knees in front of *Dadu's* body, mumbling incomprehensibly, while my uncle stood behind him, likely coordinating the travel arrangements on his phone. Walking past the kitchen, I noticed the contractor attaching rebars to the kitchen window for added security. I made my way to the dining room and caught a glimpse of my mother, the Colonel's wife, and a few of my paternal relatives in *Dadu*'s room, trying to organise the mess left behind by the robbers. I stood by the door, listening, as the Colonel's wife said, "They took everything!" Everyone else remained silent.

What is "everything"? In our culture, when a woman gets married, the husband's family is traditionally required to provide her with a specific amount of gold jewellery, as agreed upon by her family, before the marriage can proceed—A form of "reverse" dowry. Over time, and with rising living costs, this tradition evolved into more of a formal vow. In modern weddings, the concept has transformed into a written contract, similar to a prenuptial agreement, where the husband agrees to give the wife a specified sum of money during the marriage, which she can use freely. It's a practical system, especially in today's world where a large percentage of marriages end in divorce. It's a way to safeguard your assets and avoid losing your house, car, half your savings, and your last pair of untorn underwear to an ex-spouse!

In the past, though, gold was seen as an investment for the family's future. Husbands would gift their wives as much gold as they could afford, and *Dadu* was no exception. She had received a lot of gold from her husband, who passed away when he was still young. Unlike my mother, who had sold her wedding gold to support Nida's education when my father couldn't pay for it, *Dadu* never had to sell hers. She was well cared for.

If anything, I think the burglary was a blessing in disguise. Otherwise, there would have been a family feud among my paternal relatives over who deserved how much of *Dadu*'s gold. Personally, I believe my mother should have kept it all since she was the one who always took care of *Dadu*, but if I said that out loud, they might lash back with slogans about equality. I'm not saying they're bad people or that equality is wrong, but there's a fine line between equality and fairness. As humans, we tend to favour whichever movement benefits us most.

There was a life lesson somewhere in that interaction: Fairness is more important than equality.

Let me clarify before you decide to cancel me entirely: Equality is often a concept invoked by those who feel slighted by a decision they perceive as unfair. Many people receive rewards with little effort simply because they are favoured by those making the decisions, while others put in all the effort and still go unrecognised, as the system bends toward fairness for some at the expense of others in the name of equality: You'll also see how this issue becomes particularly relevant to us later on.

Two workers carried a slab of ice on an open casket out of the truck, one hauling a handle at the head side and the other at the foot. They placed the casket beside *Dadu*'s body and stood by, awaiting further instructions. Colonel Oman was a strict man who valued discipline, enforced the idea of "speak only when you are spoken to, and answer only the question you are asked." Though he wasn't intimidating, everyone felt self-conscious around him.

Finally, it was decided that all the cars would leave for Naogaon at noon. *Dadu*'s body was placed on the slab of ice, and the casket was returned to the freezer truck. The next two days would be a busy time for everyone, with only close relatives staying for a week to settle any affairs and financial dues *Dadu* might owe to locals. Surprisingly, everyone had brought packed bags, which the Colonel had communicated well in advance, leaving little room for my father to decline the trip.

As we packed up, we watched our relatives pile into their cars. We shared transport with some family members, while my mother and sister locked up the rooms behind us, leaving Chacha and Anna at home to let the contractor out after he finished securing the windows. I sat in the back of someone's car with my mother and sister, while the Oman brothers rode in the Colonel's vehicle. I turned around as we drove away from our driveway, watching Chacha and Anna close the perimeter gates behind us.

Though *Dadu*'s passing was a deeply sorrowful event, I felt a strange excitement being surrounded by so many familiar faces. A train of nine cars, with the freezer truck in the middle, travelled down the open highway, almost like a procession to Naogaon. The journey would take six hours, and I knew it would be a long, boring ride. I slept through half of it and gazed out at the scenery for the other half while listening to Nida spin stories about her studies and friends to my mother. It had been eight years since I last visited Naogaon, and I didn't realise then that it would be my last.

As dusk settled, we arrived at *Dadu*'s Naogaon residence—a four-story estate that had remained largely empty for the past decade. The only distant aunt who lived there had passed away a few years after *Dadu* moved in with us. Locals emerged from their homes to watch as the large convoy of cars approached *Dadu*'s final resting place beside her husband, my grandfather.

Families discussed their living arrangements and took rooms in the house. Soon, the once-desolate four-story building came alive with a flurry of activity as everyone pitched in to divide responsibilities—cleaning the premises, restoring power and water, and stocking up on groceries to prepare for their stay. With such a large group, it didn't take long to get settled. I played on the second floor with cousins while *Dadu*'s casket was placed in her old bedroom on that same floor. As night fell, everyone retreated to their rooms in preparation for the long day of religious rituals ahead before *Dadu* would be buried at noon.

We stayed on the fourth floor, while my father chose to spend his last night in *Dadu*'s room, lying next to his deceased mother. Curiosity got the better of me, and I hurried down the flights of stairs around midnight to see how my father had arranged himself. I felt no fear, knowing that people occupied every room. The building was laid out monotonously, with a large balcony connecting the rooms on the second floor. *Dadu's* bedroom, a corner room at the end of the balcony, was the largest in the house, befitting the former lady of the estate.

As I dashed across the balcony, I suddenly felt a chill envelop me. It was unusually cold, and as I exhaled, I could see fog forming in front of me, reminiscent of a clichéd horror movie moment before a ghost appears. Unlike a protagonist in a scary film, I didn't slow down; I quickened my pace and reached *Dadu's* bedroom door.

Upon opening it, I discovered the source of the frigid air. The air conditioner was blasting at full capacity, and the ice beneath *Dadu* was slowly melting. The workers had left several smaller slabs of ice in a large pan in the room for additional cooling. The combined effects made the space colder than the coldest winter day, while outside, it was warm and humid.

I found my father on *Dadu's* bed, gazing at her casket on the ground beside him. He looked curled up and vulnerable until he turned his gaze to me, extending a hand inviting me to join him, nodding inquisitively. "It's too cold; I'll go upstairs," I replied, and he simply nodded. I walked away, puzzled at how he remained comfortable in just a shirt and pants.

What had I just witnessed? Was that really *The* Lieutenant Oman? My father, the younger Oman, had always been *Dadu's* favourite. *Dadu* herself was born in a time when polio was rampant. She had never been vaccinated as a child, and as a result, one of her legs was significantly shorter than the other. This meant that, from an early age, she couldn't carry out household chores as efficiently as others, which made finding a suitor difficult. Yet, against the odds, my paternal grandfather, a school teacher who came from one of the wealthiest families of that era, took an interest in her and agreed to marry her.

It took me years to piece together all these details, after countless conversations with family members. I was close to *Dadu*, and during her delusional periods, she would often mistake me for my father. In one such moment, she looked at me, thinking I was him, and said, "I am happy for you. You are my pride and joy."

Even though *Dadu* had lost awareness of the present, she could vividly recall fragments of her past. I would often engage her in conversation to stimulate her memory.

"They make fun of me, Obik," she once said, using my father's first name. "They call me *lengra*"—a Bengali slang for cripple. "I wish you could come and tell them to stop."

I pressed gently, "What do you mean, *Dadu*? Who's saying that to you?"

Sobbing, she replied, "His family, everyone."

According to what Nida had once told me, my grandfather's family had never been happy with the marriage. They wanted him to marry a woman without a disability, and they made *Dadu*'s life difficult by assigning her tasks that required climbing stairs—a great challenge for her. My grandfather, however, would shield her from most of the abuse, often standing up to his own parents. She was happiest when she was with him, but after his death, she had to fend for herself and raise her sons. Left to the mercy of in-laws who resented her, she faced relentless bullying.

"Tell them, Obik," she would often say. "Tell them what you told them yesterday!" Even as a skinny, young teenager, my father would pick fights with anyone who harassed *Dadu* about her disability. He would get beaten up badly and return home bruised, only for *Dadu* to patch him up. But he was never alone. He would come back with his brother, and together, they'd wreak havoc on the bullies in the village.

"The day you left, I cried. Who will protect me now, Obik?" she said, referring to the day my father left for military training. He had been one of the top students in the officer's exam and was selected for an elite force in the Pakistan Army that only took the best. His enlistment meant leaving *Dadu* behind.

"They taunted me, Obik. They said everyone around me would leave me. When you come back, you show them! You tell them."

I asked, "Tell them what, *Dadu*?"

With emotion, she replied, "Tell them I was never alone!"

In her final days, *Dadu* was trapped in a time loop, reliving the bittersweet memory of her favourite son leaving for the military—proud of his achievement but heartbroken by his absence. Every day, she revisited that moment, and then the time she prayed endlessly for his safe return from the war.

As both brothers found success in their respective careers, the question arose of who would take care of their aging mother and give her the life she had always deserved—at least in her final years. Though her sons and inherited wealth ensured she lived in comfort in Naogaon, with all the luxuries her newfound affluence could provide, she remained completely alone. With the money her sons provided, she generously helped the families of those who had once scorned her. Some genuinely appreciated her kindness. A young man she supported by helping him set up a car repair shop next door became like a grandson to her. But for many, her wealth tied to my grandfather's lineage was the only thing that mattered. She was expected to give, not out of gratitude but out of obligation.

As the years went by, people she had once known and cared for either moved on or passed away, leaving her increasingly isolated in that grand estate. She longed to be surrounded by loved ones again, frequently asking her older son to let her live with him. While he would occasionally take her in, the stays never lasted long. At first, he'd explain that there wasn't a suitable bedroom on the ground floor of their duplex, making it difficult for her to move around. Then his wife would insist they couldn't provide the necessary supervision. It was a bitter irony that a woman of considerable wealth found herself with no one willing to take her in.

Though *Dadu* had her wealth tied up in land she wouldn't rent out and gold from her marriage that she refused to sell—the same gold that was later allegedly stolen in a break-in. Only later did the truth come to light: the land she had refused to rent out had been included in her will, designated to be divided equally among her two sons and her grandchildren. She hadn't rented it simply because she didn't want to deal with the hassle of an unruly tenant, knowing her disability and isolation would make it impossible to evict someone when necessary.

Yet, instead of understanding her reasoning, everyone focused on the bitterness that grew within her over the years. They saw her as difficult and stubborn but never looked beyond that to the deeper concerns that drove her decisions—the desire to avoid trouble in her old age, to secure a future for her family, and perhaps the fear of being even more vulnerable in a world that had already given her so many challenges.

You might be wondering, if Obik was her favourite, why didn't she just go live with him from the start? The truth is, she did. She lived with my father for a time until his industries started going bankrupt. At that point, she chose to leave, perhaps to lessen the burden. It's important to recognise that every story has three sides: mine, theirs, and the truth somewhere in between. Without concrete evidence, I'm not here to cast accusations. I'll assume that the concerns voiced by the Colonel and his wife were genuine. Although it became increasingly clear that the Colonel's wife didn't want to care for his crippled mother after a certain point. Nevertheless, the reality remained—*Dadu* was no longer truly welcomed. Despite the wealth and success of her sons, she spent her final years feeling more abandoned than ever.

This was one of the first heartfelt conversations my parents ever had. My father, feeling utterly helpless, asked my mother if she'd be okay with taking *Dadu* in. Without hesitation, my mother agreed, swearing to him that she would never make his mother feel unwelcome and would care for her as if she were her own. It was a promise she kept until the very end. Her unwavering integrity in keeping a promise left a lasting impression on my father, shaping his guiding mantra: the enormous weight of a promise and the commitment to honour it. He often instilled this principle in us, emphasizing that once a promise was made, it was not just a choice but a duty to see it through.

So, even when my father struggled financially in the early 2000s, he chose to take *Dadu* in. My mother, who came from the financially poorer background and lacked proper education compared to her sister-in-law, cared for *Dadu* with love and dedication. In turn, *Dadu* cherished my mother as if she were her own daughter. Quietly, *Dadu* would give small pieces of her wedding gold to my mother, instructing her to sell them so she could buy me books, school supplies, and toys when times were tough. She made my mother promise to keep it a secret, fearing backlash from her other son and daughter-in-law, who often preached equality but failed to grasp the situation's complexity.

Despite this, *Dadu* spent her final years under my father's roof, cared for by my mother. Neither of them received much recognition for their efforts beyond a simple "thank you," while the rest of the family focused on the equal distribution of wealth. They were devastated by the theft of her remaining gold, which they had anticipated inheriting. Meanwhile, my father was inconsolable, wracked with guilt over not being able to do enough for his mother in her final years. I saw that guilt clearly in the way he curled up next to her open casket, lost in grief and regret.

In Naogaon, the following morning, prayers were held at the local mosque, where the community gathered to remember *Dadu* one last time. Afterward, *Dadu*'s body, wrapped in a white cloth, was laid to rest next to her husband, who had passed away over 40 years earlier, beside a tombstone that had fallen into disarray. My father gently lowered her into the ground and sat there beside her lifeless body, ignoring the calls from everyone urging him to come out. It was as if their voices never reached him, his focus entirely on spending those final moments with his mother. Eventually, he climbed out, and the gravekeepers began filling the grave with the same dirt they had dug up earlier. After they planted a tree seed on top and laid the final layer of soil over *Dadu*'s resting place, my father knelt on the freshly turned earth—just as my sister would kneel years later in front of his grave, in the exact same posture.

In the afternoon, the Colonel arranged for professional caterers to prepare a feast for the entire village—or anyone who might stop by—as a tribute to *Dadu*, as she used to do the same when she was living there. They cooked an abundance of food to ensure there would be enough for all. I wanted to spend time with my cousins and play, but the opportunity never seemed to arise. Later that afternoon, some of my father's older relatives from the hometown gathered on the third-floor balcony, sipping tea prepared by one of my aunts as they reminisced about the old days.

As I peeked at them from the corner of the stairs, I overheard one say, "That's Left-ten-ant Oman's son." A man with a thick moustache looked at me and invited me to join them. I agreed, knowing I would only stay for a few minutes out of sheer boredom. They claimed to remember me as a child when they visited *Dadu* at our place and during our last trip eight years ago, but I couldn't recall any of them. The conversation involved seven people, but for the sake of simplicity—and because I genuinely have no recollection of who they were or how they looked—I will refer to them collectively as "Moustached Relative." The only detail I remember is that almost all of them sported those grand, 'generational' moustaches, the kind that noblemen or manor lords might have twirled between their fingers back in the day. So, feel free to imagine me talking to identical septuplets with matching moustaches—it's probably not far from the truth!

While I don't remember how the conversation began, I recall where it led.

Moustached relative: "Your *Dadu* was really scared for your father's safety back then."

"Back when?" I asked.

The moustached relative responded, "During the war, of course. Obik's platoon returned without him. Didn't anyone ever tell you the story?"

Me: "I don't follow. What?"

He explained that my father had been captured and treated as a prisoner of war. The authorities labelled him a traitor, accusing him of being a soldier in the Pakistan Army who had broken his vows and betrayed the country. For those unfamiliar with our history, before 1971, Pakistan was divided into two regions: East Pakistan and West Pakistan. The military was predominantly made up of soldiers from the west, and those from the east, including my father, were few and far between. East Pakistan later won its independence, becoming Bangladesh, my homeland. The Oman brothers, along with a handful of others from East Pakistan, had been allowed to join the Pakistan Army before the liberation war.

Bangladesh and Pakistan had been at odds over political issues for years, which had sparked several rebellions. Most of Bangladesh's population were farmers, untrained in warfare and largely illiterate. On the night of 25th March 1971, to send a message and assert control, the Pakistani soldiers massacred an entire village of farmers in their sleep, a brutal act called *Operation Searchlight*. This act ignited the country's resolve, forcing the people to take up arms in defence. The call for help went out to anyone who could fight, and the Oman brothers were among the first to rally East Pakistani soldiers, urging them to abandon their posts. As platoons began moving eastward, they joined the Bangladeshi front, where friends and family were desperately waiting for aid.

"How did he get caught?" I asked, genuinely curious.

The moustached relative replied, "This is your uncle, Mahmoud Oman's account. At some point during their journey, they were ambushed by an opposition squad. They were outnumbered and outgunned. But Obik recognised the insignia and the squad leader—Brigadier Jawaad. Jawaad was an old friend of Obik's from Pakistan. When he saw Obik leading the platoon, they both stopped and spoke like civil human beings. Obik knew that fighting would end badly for them, so he struck a deal with Jawaad. He offered to surrender on the condition that his men be set free. The platoon was large enough to be a valuable asset to his people so he decided to sacrifice himself to save many. To Jawaad's credit, he wasn't an unreasonable man. He didn't want unnecessary bloodshed and figured that capturing the lieutenant would satisfy mission control. They needed someone to answer for state treason, and that was enough. Obik went willingly and told his brother to lead the squad out of danger and not look back."

After absorbing all this, I paused before asking, "Why would Jawaad just let an entire platoon go join the enemy?"

The moustached relative answered thoughtfully, "I'd imagine not everyone was a monster. Those in political power may have been, but no one is born evil. Everyone has loved ones, even Jawaad."

"No one is born evil," I repeated in my thoughts.

Moustached relative added: "It took your *Dadu* and your uncle two years of bureaucratic negotiations to secure your father's release long after the war had ended."

I asked, "Why did it take 2 years?"

The relative responded, "The authorities claimed they had no idea Left-ten-ant Oman had surrendered and been taken captive in the first place! They pinned it on Jawaad's platoon going rogue, suggesting it was some personal vendetta against the Oman brothers. As absurd as it sounded at the time, none of us dug deeper into the why or how. Honestly, we were just relieved he was alive and returned to us. Obik never talked about it afterwards and we respected his decision."

"So where did they find him in the end?" I asked.

The moustached relative began recounting how poorly my father had been treated in captivity—a reality I now interpret as torture. "I can't give you all the specifics, but from what we were told, him and a few other high-profile prisoners were recovered from makeshift prisons inside caves. The prisoners were kept in tiny rooms barely half their height. He spent most of the day hunched down because they couldn't stand up straight. Their legs would go numb, but there wasn't enough room to even lie down properly, so he'd curl up on the floor. When he wasn't in that cell, they tortured him in other ways."

"That would explain his hunched back and why he preferred sleeping on the storeroom floor," I thought—a reality I now interpret as post-traumatic stress disorder.

"When he came home, he couldn't stand up straight anymore," the moustached relative continued, confirming my suspicions. "Even years later, he retained that posture from being confined in such small spaces."

My curiosity getting the best of me, I asked, "Why did they keep him alive after the war?"

The relative hesitated before responding, unsure but still willing to share his theory. "I'm not certain. The thing is, they couldn't beat him too badly or kill him after the war had ended. Any visible scars or marks on his body could have caused political issues. Only your father didn't know that the war ended on 16 December."

"How he was tortured if he wasn't physically beaten," I pressed.

The moustached relatives exchanged uneasy glances, unsure of how to explain. Finally, one of them spoke cautiously, "Torture and abuse aren't always physical. But you're too young to fully understand that now. Just remember, abuse doesn't have to leave visible signs. It can be emotional or even sexual, and sometimes there are no obvious indicators at all. When a person is starved, malnourished, or isolated, they often don't fight back. They become desensitised to the horrors around them, making the abuse harder to recognise."

"Your father went back to service with the Bangladesh army soon after he regained his strength and was able to walk," the man added. "With each passing year, people around here saw him less and less."

"Why did he go straight back into service? Why didn't he take a break?" I asked.

"You'd have to ask him that," he replied, "but I doubt he'll ever give you a straight answer. A lot of his friends—people he cared about—were dead. My best guess? He blamed himself for not being here to defend them."

I quickly followed up, "Then what made him leave the army?"

The relative fell silent, smiling faintly before looking away. He knew the answer, but it was clear he didn't want to tell me. As the conversation began to stall, I seized the moment to ask, "What was he like before the war?"

The moustached relatives smiled fondly, a glint of mischief in their eyes. "He was a lovely young lad—smart as a whip, but a bit of a menace! He and his brother used to climb the neighbours' trees and swipe mangos. Now, I'm not saying stealing is good, but let's be honest, those mangos would've just spoiled anyway. He'd pick a few, and before you knew it, he was sharing them with the neighbourhood kids. We all adored him. He wasn't just pretending to care—he genuinely did!"

Before I could say anything, he continued, leaning in as if revealing a secret. "Did you know your grandfather was a school teacher? A well-respected man. He'd often try to set your father straight, even give him a good beating when he stepped out of line. But your father, he'd just sit there, take the punishment quietly—and then go right back to his mischief!" The group erupted into laughter, the memory still vivid after all these years.

I felt lost in the story, and it must have shown. "How is any of this relevant?" I asked, more confused than curious.

"Well, you wanted to know the man, didn't you? This is who he was," he said, making a fair point.

I nodded, signalling him to continue.

"When your grandfather passed away from a stroke, Obik couldn't hold back his tears. He was heartbroken. For all his antics, he was soft-hearted, always cared too much. We didn't know how he'd ever make it through military service, let alone survive and come back from war." The relative's voice softened, as though even the memory carried weight.

Intrigued, I pressed on. "And what happened after he joined the military?"

He sighed. "Even then, whenever he came home on leave, he would do whatever he could for the village—fixing roofs, building shelters, even helping folks find lost cows! He always looked out for others."

But then his tone darkened, now filled with sadness. "But after they brought him back from the war... he was different."

"Different how?" I asked.

He hesitated before speaking. "He picked up bad habits—things you're probably too young to understand."

I nodded, though I knew I'd just ask Nida later. She never put an age restriction on what I could know likely because she never had one put on her.

The moustached relative wasn't finished. "One day, your father arrived in a military vehicle to let us know that he was leaving for Dhaka. After that, we saw less and less of him. Eventually, he stopped coming back altogether."

Sensing the conversation was getting too heavy for me, he softened. "Ah, but we won't bore you with any more of that. Go, find your cousins and do whatever kids your age do."

What I had expected to be a brief interaction had turned into a conversation that left me with more questions than answers—and much to reflect on.

After Bangladesh gained its independence, many military personnel received rewards and benefits, and many, including my father, left to establish their own industries. I often wonder if he ever received the help he needed to recover from his experiences. Nida later confirmed that he developed a penchant for drinking and other vices, hints that the moustached relative dropped during our conversation. Was this why his family tolerated him? I will never know, as most of his family passed away, and I have no desire to unearth painful memories with those who remain.

Ever since we returned home from Naogaon, things grew quieter. Anna left after completing her contract that included caring for *Dadu* until her passing; I was genuinely upset to see her go. The fights between my parents grew more intense with each passing day, and my mother's health began to deteriorate rapidly. Her plans to leave crumbled under the weight of her illness and the relentless cycle of conflict. She seemed to surrender to her circumstances, enduring the bruises and blows that marked every heated argument, as her spirit faded a little more each time.

By this time, she had secluded herself to the extent that she had stopped speaking to everyone altogether, who began to grow concerned—though not suspicious, just worried.

This was the first time I heard him say to her, "I think it's okay for your family to come over for a change. I'm sure they miss you a lot," I was stunned. My father had never spoken so openly or accommodatingly about her family before. When they eloped and got married, he had insisted she sever all ties with them, as they had strongly opposed the match. To them, the Lieutenant was too old for her, and their daughter deserved better. Coming from a lower-middle-class family, they measured success by conventional standards: a government job, a career in medicine, or engineering. Businessmen and entrepreneurs, like my father, were considered unreliable and risky as suitors.

To show he was serious, my father went to a nearby furniture store on the highway and bought brand-new pieces to replace the broken, termite-infested furniture in our room. But it was too little, too late—a band-aid over a gaping wound. By then, my mother had already become mostly bedridden with the old bruises taking longer to heal than before, making it impossible for her to invite her family to see her. On the bright side, at least the constant fighting stopped.

My father began going out of his way to bring home some of the best doctors in the city to examine her, but none ever found any physical ailments outside of the non-healing bruises. He reached out to local herbalists and resorted to homeopathic pseudoscience when medical doctors were unable to help. My mother's condition continued to deteriorate, and the sugar pills prescribed by the homeopathic "doctor" did nothing to improve her health.

I remember marking the date on the calendar on my study table so I wouldn't forget—the day she passed away quietly in her sleep as Nida and I desperately tried to wake her. My father wasn't home, and he had sent Chacha on some errand, leaving just Nida and me to stay with her lifeless body for hours until he returned. When he finally arrived, he took her away to be buried in a graveyard of his choosing without notifying anyone.

To this day, I've never met my maternal family. I doubt they even know their daughter passed away all those years ago.

Chapter 5. Generosity

I blamed my father for what he had done to my mother, and after she passed, he never once mentioned her again. I was too afraid to even look him in the eye, unsure of how he might react if I upset him. He started traveling to Pirojpur less, choosing instead to stay home with us, but his presence was far from comforting. He hired a new maid to help us with the cooking and household choirs.

My silence at the dinner table seemed to agitate him. He would tell stories and wait for me to laugh along, but I never did. I was a mess in every sense. I couldn't even separate chicken or fish from its bones, often leaving my plate untouched. My room was no better—dust and filth piled up everywhere, turning it into a reflection of my inner turmoil. Despite Chacha and the maid offering to clean, I refused to let anyone into the space that I shared with my mother. It was as if keeping the room in disarray gave me a sense of control over something in my life. My father often directed his frustration at Chacha and the maid, blaming them for my unruliness, though they would insist they were doing their best—and they truly were. The truth was, I was simply being difficult. At the dinner table, he would launch into lectures about discipline, trying to drill it into me, but I refused to acknowledge his words. When his frustration reached a breaking point, my sister would step in to diffuse the tension, saying things like, "Father, let it go, please."

This became a pattern—tension at breakfast, lunch, and dinner—until one day, he finally snapped and said to Nida. "I don't know how his mother raised him, and I don't know how he'll survive on his own!"

I had always kept my anger bottled up, but this time, I couldn't hold back. "I wouldn't have to worry about surviving if you hadn't killed her in the first place," I blurted out. The words escaped my mouth before I even realized what I had said.

71

His face turned red with fury, and I could feel the rage building. Before he could act, Nida quickly intervened, placing a calming hand on his shoulder. "Don't pay him any heed, Father," she said softly. He listened to her, of course—he always did. She was his favourite. Anything she said could quiet him, though I knew he would take it out on me or my mother later, if she were still alive. As I sat there, shaking with anger and fear, I couldn't help but think that the next time when Nida wasn't there, he might actually beat me to death.

In a twisted attempt to make amends, my father started buying me clothes and other things I didn't need. He would insist I wear the new clothes he bought, and his agitation would grow if I didn't. I never cared much for new clothes; I was perfectly comfortable with the few I already had. To me, his gestures felt less like care and more like an attempt to buy my affection, and I resented it.

His actions at the time were something similar to how lonely, misguided men shower gifts on so-called 'content creators' they meet online nowadays—women they don't know personally but believe they can win over with expensive presents. While these men think their gifts will earn the woman's love, all they're really doing is funding her lifestyle, her vacations with a boyfriend, or her bills. Social media and e-commerce have made it easier than ever to scale this dynamic, replacing what used to be physical labour with a more global, digital exchange, which too leads absolutely nowhere for the desperate men.

I became increasingly vigilant around my father. One afternoon, Nida and Chacha were supposed to return from her tutor's home, but they were running an hour late. It was almost dinner time, and father kept calling their phones, but neither answered. His head trembled, and he began pacing around the driveway near the perimeter gates, ready to go out looking for them. The tension in the air was suffocating. Then, suddenly, the gate lock clicked open, and Nida and Chacha walked in.

"Where were you?" my father snapped at Nida, his voice sounding less concerned and more irritated.

Nida, visibly shaken, replied, "We were mugged on the way back. A few men stopped our rickshaw in a dark alley and made us get off."

His tone shifted, now laced with concern. "Are you hurt? Did they hurt you?"

Nida quickly explained, "No, they just snatched my bag and my phone and threatened the rickshaw puller with a knife."

Father turned to Chacha, clearly frustrated. "What were you doing?"

Chacha slurred under the influence of Gul, "Sir, I was terrified... They said to hand everything over, so I complied."

Nida chuckled nervously, adding, "They were only focused on me. Chacha just handed his phone over voluntarily. Even the muggers were surprised by how proactive Chacha was in being their best victim of the year." Her sarcasm, though light-hearted, was oddly entertaining.

Recalling the events seemed to offer Nida some relief, but my father didn't share her sense of ease. He told Nida to go to her room, which she quietly obeyed. Chacha and my father stood there, speaking in hushed tones I couldn't quite make out. Nida walked past me, subtly signalling me to go to my room. Naturally, I ignored her, driven by curiosity. After what felt like an eternity of low-volume conversation, my father slapped Chacha with such force that he flew across the driveway, crashing face-first into the ground. I froze in terror, paralysed by the fear that he might kill Chacha.

In that moment, a vivid flashback hit me—one of my mother being beaten in the same brutal manner. Panic set in as I raced to the landline in the dining room. My hands shook as I dialled the police, my voice trembling as I desperately tried to explain that my father was beating someone to death, providing our address.

Rushing back outside, I saw my father standing over Chacha, who was crying on the ground. I didn't have the courage to intervene. Instead, I ran to Nida's room and told her that I informed the police and that we'll be saved soon.

"You did what?!" she exclaimed.

I didn't understand what I had done wrong. How could I stand by and let him kill someone else?

Nida told me to stay inside her room while she ran outside to handle the situation. The heated argument that followed was terrifying. I could hear their voices rising, and father's footsteps echoed as he approached her bedroom door. My heart pounded in my chest as I stood on the other side of it. But Nida managed to calm him down, and soon the sound of sirens filled the air. My father reluctantly walked out to meet the officer who had arrived in response to the call.

I walked outside and saw my father, Nida, and Chacha standing with the police officer. The siren had drawn the attention of the neighbours, who gathered at the perimeter gate, curious about the commotion.

"Lieutenant, is everything in order?" the officer asked my father, to which he replied, "Yes, just a bit of an argument that got out of hand."

The officer pressed on, "The call was about someone being beaten." He looked at Chacha's swollen face and red, tear-streaked eyes. Then, addressing Chacha directly, he asked, "Do you have anything to say about that?"

To my surprise, Chacha nodded and said, "No sir, everything is fine."

At that moment, I couldn't understand why he would defend my father and not report the truth.

The officer left, and my father walked inside first, brushing past me. All he muttered was, "Be careful that this doesn't happen again."

Soon after, my father also bought a secondhand Toyota SE Salon at an auction identical to the one he crashed. I thought to myself, "*A creature of habit*". Travelling by car was definitely safer for Nida, especially at that age when she was vulnerable to catcalling on the streets—and, as recent trends have shown, even the risk of being mugged. This time, a chauffeur sat in the driver's seat while my father would occupy the back. I suppose he could never bring himself to get behind the wheel after the accident.

For my Western readers, hiring a chauffeur in Bangladesh is far more accessible than in Australia or America, where it's typically reserved for the ultra-wealthy. In developing economies like Bangladesh in the early part of the 21st century, the primary focus wasn't efficiency but job creation, as there were no fixed minimum wages tied to specific employment categories. Becoming a chauffeur was a viable option for those without formal education who sought a better life than working as a farmer where a year of bad harvest paid no wages at all. The only real requirement was learning how to drive.

While many skilled drivers chose this profession, the pre-digitisation era exposed the country to widespread corruption. Some individuals obtained licenses by paying bribes to government officials, bypassing any formal driving tests or experience. This practice, though drastically diminished, still persists today, albeit mostly benefiting the wealthy and well-connected, whose children or employees acquire licenses without ever taking a test or properly learning how to drive.

Does that inherently make them bad drivers? Not necessarily. After five years on the road, many would appear competent, reinforcing the notion that experience can trump formal certification. This isn't entirely unlike remote areas in Australia or America, where underage children are sometimes allowed to drive, a practice treated as an open secret—acceptable, as long as no one gets hurt.

My father completely stopped speaking to me. Meals were eaten in complete silence, with my father ignoring my presence entirely. One afternoon, the Colonel came to visit. My father instructed the maid to prepare tea and serve it to the guest. On her way, she accidentally dropped the tray and a china teapot that my mother had received many years ago. The teapot was from the baby boomer generation that accumulated more china than they knew what to do with. They rarely had enough guests to justify the vast quantities of china, yet they ate off plastic and metal dishes at home, staring at the carefully displayed china in showcases. It was the same generation that passed down these seemingly precious items as "inheritance" to children who would later sell the utensils at the local thrift store.

To us, it was just a broken teapot and spilled tea. But my father snapped. He walked up to the maid, grabbed her by her hair bun, and demanded an explanation. I was terrified, but at least the Colonel was there. Yet, to my surprise, all he said was, "Obik, that's enough!" My father backed off, but the maid was visibly shaken. She slowly cleaned up the mess, tears streaming down her face.

That evening, after the Colonel left, the landlord came to collect the rent, and my father sent me out to tell him my usual line: "Father isn't home, come back tomorrow!" But this time, I whispered, "Father is hurting people. Please help!" The landlord paused, looked at me, and said, "Don't worry, child. I'll be right back." He left.

My father saw him leave from the roof and thought that I had done as I was instructed.

An hour later, the landlord returned with the police. He had filed a report saying that Lieutenant Oman was abusing his children and was "not an upstanding tenant and should be evicted." It wasn't about helping us—it was a way for the landlord to rid himself of a tenant who wouldn't pay rent on time.

The police took my father in handcuffs and instructed Chacha to lock the door behind them. As they left, I couldn't help but think: no wonder Chacha stayed silent. Silence, it seems, can be bought—if the price is right, or if the cost of speaking out is too high.

Even then, I knew the police wouldn't keep him in for long. If it happened today, I'd imagine he'd spend the night in the station alongside other parents falsely accused of abduction under Amber Alerts—cases where bitter ex-partners misuse the legal system, reporting a co-parent simply for being late returning from a trip to the carnival, fuelled more by petty personal grudges than genuine concern.

Father returned from the police station the next morning, having been bailed out by Colonel. He was furious with me and stood outside on the driveway, screaming for me to come out. Nida heard the commotion and rushed over. I stood at my bedroom door, trembling, unsure of what to do. Nida quickly approached me and said, "I'll take care of this. But please, for my sake, stop doing this. There's a time and place to be vocal, and this isn't it."

She ran outside to console him, leaving me behind to listen from where I stood. I could hear fragments of their heated exchange, like when my father shouted, "We're being evicted with only two weeks' notice, right when I'm about to close the deal for Pirojpur with Hossein. That ungrateful brat is actively trying to ruin me. I should kick him out and let him fend for himself. Maybe then he'll learn to appreciate the life he *had* with family support enabling his reckless behaviour."

Nida pleaded, "You're being irrational and I'm not enabling him. He's just a child."

Father bellowed, "You were his age too when your mother left, and you still chose me. You didn't go stabbing me in the back."

At that, Nida broke down, her voice trembling as she pleaded, "Please don't take him away too. I'll be all alone again. I promise he won't do it again—just this once, do it for me."

Father's tone softened slightly, but his words remained cutting: "Nida, you're testing my patience."

She begged again, "Please!" Their conversation continued in muffled tones that I couldn't fully make out from where I stood. However, I clearly heard my father's final words:

"Fine. But make sure the boy never steps out of line again. Now, I need to find us another place to live."

On his way in, he called for the maid. She hurried toward him as he said, "Police orders. We're to let you go. Take your final payment and pack up—leave by the end of today."

The maid mumbled, "But sir, please... no! I have a child at home."

At that moment, I found it strange that she was pleading to stay. After all, hadn't I saved her from the torture? The thing is, we often endure circumstances we dislike to support our loved ones. It's a choice, not a force. Our maid was likely concerned about how she would feed her child if dismissed on the spot, since the wages they earned were barely enough to get by, let alone save for a rainy day. This kind of work was known as "daily wages for daily expenses."

Two weeks later, we moved to a smaller apartment that father rented a few blocks down the road. He sent off all the furniture he bought for mother before we moved to Pirojpur, meaning my room now lay barren too as we shared the same room. He never mentioned any of my past "transgressions", and I honoured Nida's request by doing the same.

My father had sent Chacha ahead a week earlier to prepare the place, making sure the gas lines, electricity fixtures, and furnitures were set up before our arrival. Chacha assured us everything was ready, though Nida had a sneaking suspicion that what he really meant was he'd found the perfect crevice in the apartment to stash his gul. The apartment door creaked open, and my father stepped inside, flicking on the lights as he entered. I followed close behind, dragging the heavier of my two suitcases, while Nida trailed after me, struggling with the lighter one. Without saying a word, my father gestured for me to follow—not down the main corridor where the bedrooms were, but left, through the living space, toward a small room tucked away in the far corner. I didn't give it much thought at first, recalling how Nida's room in our old house had also been set apart from the rest of us.

He opened the door and switched on the light, revealing what had once been a small guest room, now converted into a storage space. A small bed with bed posts not higher than one foot off the ground lay against the wall with a torn mattress on top. A wooden clothing rack was positioned next to it which held a few old shirts and pants. I stared at it, trying to make sense of the situation, when my father broke the silence, "That's not for you. That's Chacha's."

Chacha had made this room his, living among the cargo boxes. After a brief pause, my father decided, "Move it outside, next to your door." The bed frame wasn't too heavy, so I managed to drag it out unassisted. I placed it by the door as instructed. I couldn't help but think that Chacha wouldn't be too thrilled with the new arrangement when he comes back from whatever errand father had sent him on. I also moved his clothing rack out of the room, leaving behind stacks of containers and cargo boxes. My father glanced at them and said, "I'll have these sent to Pirojpur tomorrow."

I was still wondering where I would sleep, now that the room was stripped of even its makeshift bed. I briefly considered stacking some of the cargo boxes to create a makeshift bed for the night when my father spoke again, "Walk with me."

We left the apartment in silence, stepping out into the street. The new house was still in Uttara, but on the opposite side of the highway that cut through the neighbourhood—an area more developed, where the last remnants of farmland were being swallowed by new construction. As we walked, my father made an odd squeaking sound by pressing his lips together and releasing air from one side, like someone smoking a cigar. I hadn't noticed him do that before, but it stuck with me.

On the way, I passed rows of roadside food stalls, bustling with students who had likely just finished their tutoring sessions, and white-collar workers with wrinkled, untucked shirts indicating that they had wrapped up gruelling 9-to-9 shifts. Despite their different backgrounds, they sat and dined together, unified by hunger and the convenience of the stalls. The shopping complexes along the route, which in my childhood only sold nuts and screws for fixing broken wardrobe panels, had been replaced by larger dine-in eateries and stores that sold imported goods. Uttara was developing at a rapid pace, driven by rapid urbanisation and the high concentration of Western-curriculum schools and colleges.

After walking a couple of kilometres, we finally arrived at a roadside furniture store. You might wonder, who keeps a furniture stall open so late? You'd have a point! It's something I noticed when I first arrived in Australia, where most places closed by 5:00 pm on weekdays, except for a few select shops and streets that stayed open until 9:00 pm, and only for food or entertainment. But in Dhaka, if it's self-run, it stays open until people stop coming or the owner collapses—whichever comes first.

The shopkeeper who was also the owner sold my father the first set of furniture that he purchased for our old house, the ones that he sent to me later. Yet, he approached us with a nervous energy.

"H-How can I help, sir?" he stuttered.

My father's eyes shifted toward me, prompting the shopkeeper to follow his gaze. "Mokbul, the boy needs a bed," he said, his voice as cold and detached as ever.

The shopkeeper looked at me with a brief flicker of confusion that I didn't fully understand. Without further questions, he began showing me several single metal bed frames. I picked one, and my father gave Mokbul a subtle nod of approval. The shopkeeper, now visibly tense, quickly dismantled the frame and wrapped it up, adding a light mattress at my father's request. He loaded everything onto a trolley, or "*thela gari*," as I had mentioned before. Despite having a motor vehicle parked nearby, he opted for the trolley, likely because he knew the distance wasn't far and wanted to save on fuel.

At the time, I thought, "*I wouldn't blame you for being nervous around the Lieutenant*"

Half an hour passed, and I stood there watching as Mokbul laid out his tools and placed the pieces of the bed frame in the centre of my new room. He sat on the floor, preparing to assemble it, but then paused, glancing up at me with an expectant look that I didn't fully understand at first.

"Don't just stand there. Help me set it up. It'll go much faster that way," he said.

Puzzled, I responded, "But I've never done this before."

He sighed, realising that I probably hadn't had much experience with basic tasks around the house. "Come, I'll show you," he said, motioning for me to join him.

Meanwhile, my father, who had been standing by the door, leaning against the frame with one leg crossed over the other, straightened up. "I'll leave him with you," he told the shopkeeper before walking away to his bedroom, leaving me behind.

Mokbul seemed compelled to justify why he insisted on teaching me basic tasks. "It's always good to learn basic life skills, even if it's someone else's job to do them. Don't be the 'it's *their* job' type of person all the time—it just makes you difficult to work with," he explained.

I nodded and replied, "You make a valid point."

Encouraged, Mokbul continued, "What I found was that when I understood every inch of my trade, I could manage my assistants more efficiently without stressing them out. So my advice doesn't just stop at life skills—it's a professional recommendation too, especially if you're a contractor or planning to run your own business."

For the next while, I worked alongside Mokbul, handing him tools, holding pieces steady, and learning how to put the bed together. To my surprise, I actually enjoyed it. I felt useful for the first time in a long time, like I was contributing to something, even if it was just setting up a bed.

As I tightened bolts and aligned the frame, a small sense of accomplishment welled up inside me. It was something I'd never done before, but here I was, learning and making progress. In that moment, I felt positive, like maybe I had made the right choice after all.

It didn't take long to finish setting up the bed. As I stood up, I noticed that the man had a habit of branding his furniture with cheap sticker logos. This one, in particular, read "Mokbul Furnitures," the name of his store. "Ugh!" I muttered in distaste, attempting to peel it off while Mokbul wasn't looking, but all it did was leave a sticky residue on the frame. Frustrated, I decided to leave it on—choosing the lesser of two evils.

Once we were done, Mokbul walked over and knocked on my father's bedroom door. My father emerged wearing a t-shirt and his signature sarong, asking, "Done?"

Mokbul nodded nervously, collected his payment, and quietly left.

Without acknowledging me, my father called for the live-in maid, who emerged from the quarters behind the kitchen. His tone with the help was as harsh as ever. She was a new face, almost as if she had come with the apartment. In reality, my father had hired her shortly before we moved in to help make the transition smoother, particularly with food and laundry—much like how a military quartermaster ensures everything is in order before personnel arrive at a new post.

"Put food on the table." he ordered.

The maid knew better than to ask questions and simply replied, "Right away, sir."

In the meantime, my father used the intercom that connected to the parking lot downstairs and instructed our chauffeur, Mizan, to come upstairs, hand over the car keys, and take his leave for the night.

Within minutes, the doorbell rang. My father opened it, took the car keys from the chauffeur, and sent him on his way. By the time the door shut, the maid, nearly out of breath, had finished setting the table, laying out the warmed food in record time.

The three of us sat at the dinner table—my father at the head, Nida on one side, and myself on the other. My father sat hunched over, as usual, but this time with a slight tremor in his movements, subtle but constant. It took me a moment to remember where I'd last seen him like this—right, the night he fought off that thief on the roof and sat in *Dadu*'s room afterward. Back then, I thought it was just fatigue or frustration with his relatives. Nida didn't seem too bothered, so I brushed it off as well.

On the table was the familiar spread: rice, lentil dahl, vegetables, fried fish, and chicken—all cooked in the morning and cycled through the day's meals. This was what we had since mother passed away.

Before we started eating, my father handed the car keys to Nida and said, "Let Mizan know when to come tomorrow." Then he turned to me and asked, "Do you think you're old enough to travel on your own?"

Nida simply rolled her eyes.

For some reason, my throat dried up at this seemingly harmless question. "Yes," I managed to reply.

"Good," he said, "Tomorrow, we'll get a few new things for your room. I'll leave for Pirojpur after everything's paid for. You can handle the deliveries and set up your new room."

It was strange but welcome. In the past, he would've never let me out of the house, and now he was giving me responsibilities. I'll admit, it felt good.

Then, out of nowhere, he said. "Nida's agreed to share *her* car with you, and I'm fine with that."

I hesitated but wanted clarification. "Her car?"

His expression was dead as he gave a thin, blank smile that sent a chill through me. "Yes, the car is in her name. She chose me over her mother, so she deserves it. You've never had to make such a difficult choice, yet you never missed an opportunity stab me in the back!"

There was some truth to that, but I bit my tongue, choosing not to argue. He was letting me use the car, and that was enough.

I finished my meal in silence while my father ate very quickly, almost as if his life depended on it, leaving his dirty plate on the table. He walked to the sink to wash his hands, instructing the maid to clear his plate. Back when Mother was alive, she made sure I cleaned up after myself, so watching someone else do it felt strange. But I stayed quiet as the maid took it away. It's a shame that most of my colleagues at work don't understand the basic manners of cleaning the utensils and bowls they take from the common pantry, leaving dirty dishes unwashed in the sink. Or maybe they all grew up motherless!

Nida was always a slow eater and remained at the table, quietly eating long after I was done and my plate had been cleared. I stood up to wash my hands and, as I turned around, saw her sitting there alone, taking her time with each bite at that big, empty table.

Instead of heading straight to my room after washing my hands, I made a different choice. I walked back to the table and sat down next to her, joining her in the quiet company of the evening.

"You don't have to wait for me," she said.

"I know. I still want to," I replied.

She smiled, her usual warmth breaking through. "Sorry about your living arrangements."

"Don't be silly," I said, "I'm lucky to have a room at all. I was ready to sleep on the floor if I had the choice!" teasing her about what father said moments before.

We joked and laughed until she finished her meal, then playfully shooed me away. I laughed with her. Afterwards, we headed to our rooms.

As I passed Chacha's bed near my door, I called out with a grin, "Chacha isn't going to like this."

Without turning around, Nida replied, "All Chacha cares about is his stash of gul."

We both smiled. "But why is he still here?" I asked, genuinely curious. "I get that our previous home was big enough, but why bring him along here too?"

She paused as she opened her door. "Dunno. But I think he'll stay with us until one of us dies—probably me before him! He'll outlive us all."

I chuckled and stepped into my room as I heard her door close behind her. I closed mine with a soft click.

When I woke up the next morning, I had missed school again. This had been almost every other day since my mother passed. It didn't bother me much though, and my father didn't seem too upset either. Maybe I'd give myself a free pass for today? After all, we had to buy furniture to make my room feel like home. Honestly, I was excited.

I got ready before stepping out of my room. As I opened the door, I saw Chacha lying on the bed I had set up near my doorstep the night before. He was back from wherever father had sent him. He greeted me with his toothless grin, looking anything but confused or upset. I couldn't help but smile back. His warmth was contagious. He was a sweet, short, old gul-addict; I loved his company!

"I hope you are well, Yaad!" he exclaimed, and that simple bit of concern was all I had been looking for since mother passed.

The maid was setting up breakfast on the table. In our family, we always started the day with rice instead of bread or paratha, something quick, simple, and easy to reheat. The maid, Shahana, was young, probably no older than twenty, with a bright, welcoming smile.

"Sir, breakfast is ready," she said, flashing her smile. "Shall I go get sir and miss?"

"Sir?" I asked curiously.

Shahana fumbled, "Yes, the Left-ten-ant... senior sir asked to start addressing you as Sir and get your permission on things when Miss Nida is unavailable."

I was taken aback—someone asking *me* for permission? My chest puffed up a little as I tried to sound authoritative. "Please do!" I replied, though my attempt at command sounded a bit clumsy.

Shahana nodded, "Right away," and went to knock on my father's and sister's doors. After a few knocks, they both answered, and Shahana cheerfully repeated, "Breakfast is ready!"

She was energetic and efficient, a rare quality, especially in someone working such long hours.

After breakfast, we headed downstairs.

We both got into the back seat of a car. "Give me a list of the things you need urgently," my father said as Mizan backed us out of the driveway.

"Well, I was hoping to have my Playstation back which you sent to Pirojpur along with the rest of mother's things. Could we maybe go pick it up?" I asked hopefully.

He turned to me and smiled, "Let's buy you something new instead. My son should only have the best!"

It felt insincere, almost performative. Instead of ever apologising, he seemed to be overcompensating—like a man weighed down by guilt, yet simultaneously ensuring I knew I'd never measure up to Nida. He was a weird man!

With that, he instructed Mizan to take us to the largest tech mall in the city. True to his word, he took me to a computer store and gave me a budget to pick out some decent parts for a new desktop. I was overjoyed.

We returned to the same furniture store, and as our car pulled up, the shopkeeper immediately recognised us. He emerged with the same nervous energy as the last time, visibly anxious as my father stepped out of the car.

"Come, let's leave the computer parts in the car and sort out your furniture now. I need to pay the man and head out," he said. "I trust you can handle the rest?"

His faith in me made me feel both proud and responsible. "Yes, sir!" I replied eagerly.

My father, though dressed casually at home, always made a point to look sharp when he went out—designer shirts scented with Old Spice cologne, crisp pants, leather boots, a distinctive thin silver chain resting around his neck, and Ray-Ban sunglasses. He didn't look like just another customer. He looked like he owned the place. His presence alone had a way of unsettling people, even me, and I could understand why the shopkeeper was on edge

"Show him his options," my father ordered the shopkeeper, who immediately led me inside to browse the store's tightly packed selection of tables and wardrobes, stacked high to save space. I chose a simple wardrobe, a table, and a chair—nothing extravagant, just what I needed. I think my father appreciated my practical choices.

He called the shopkeeper by name, beckoning him with a subtle hand gesture. The man hurried over, where they exchanged a few hushed words. My father then pulled a bundle of cash from his back pocket, peeled off several banknotes, and handed them over. The shopkeeper responded with an awkward military-style salute, which my father met with an icy stare. Clearly rattled, the shopkeeper dropped the salute, offering a more humble nod of gratitude.

Approaching me, my father said, "It's all paid for. He'll write you a receipt. Take it and the car. I've told Chacha to move the boxes from your room, and he'll hand them over to a guy who will deliver them to Pirojpur. He'll follow you with the furniture after it's loaded. Once he and his boys set everything up, let them leave. Oh and boy...Don't waste time talking to him."

I tried to absorb the barrage of instructions but only managed to say, "Yes, father!" He turned and walked off, disappearing down the nearest street in a rickshaw.

The shopkeeper then led me to his office at the back of the store, motioning for me to sit while he prepared the receipt. As he worked, Mokbul asked, "What's the billing address for this purchase? Which house is this going to?"

Momentarily confused, I realised he must be thinking of our old house. He'd delivered furniture to us before.

"We don't stay at the house in Sector 4 anymore," I corrected him. "There's just one now."

He paused, looking puzzled. "The Left-ten-ant told me you'd moved out of Sector 4, but even so, I've got two active addresses in my records."

I was baffled. "Two? You mean you also have the Pirojpur address?"

"No...in Uttara"

Then, as if he'd realised something, he quickly shifted his tone. "I'll just bill it to the house where I delivered the bed yesterday. Sign here, and we'll follow you."

That felt strange, but I brushed it off, assuming he'd made a mistake with the addresses. We both stepped out of the office to finalise the arrangements. The delivery was uneventful and went as expected.

As the morning shifted into afternoon, I finished setting up my room and my new computer. To my horror, every one of the furnitures had the unsightly "Mokbul Furnitures" sticker affixed onto them. But at this point, there was little else to do—when the product itself isn't up to par, you compensate by turning up the volume on the marketing.

There was a small window in the corner that let in just the right amount of sunlight, and I positioned my bed to face it. It felt good to sit in the sun and do absolutely nothing for a while. In the background, I heard Nida leaving the house, likely headed to her tutor's after school. The hurried footsteps that followed her belonged to Chacha, trailing behind as the door clicked shut behind them both.

My father had insisted that Chacha and the car always accompany Nida whenever she left the house, never trusting her alone with the chauffeur. Although too old to be a bodyguard, Chacha was dubbed "Father's spy" by Nida—a nickname she found hilarious, especially since she joked that he'd probably outlive us all! Chacha's job was to re-port back everything my sister did, but his version of events was often clouded by his habit of chewing Gul, which made my father take his reports with more than a grain of salt.

At the time, my teenage self didn't see anything wrong with this arrangement. In fact, I envied Nida for the constant company, the car rides, and the sense of importance it all seemed to carry. I thought that's why I moved in with my father—to live that kind of life. Instead, I was still taking rickshaws most places, a reality I hadn't fully matured enough to appreciate. Yet I never noticed that when I availed the car, Nida took Chacha and happily travelled by rickshaw.

School wasn't any easier than before since mother passed away. I faced constant bullying—taunts and jeers aimed at my social awkwardness that made me an easy target. Not all the kids were mean, but the voices of the few who were, seemed to drown out the kindness of everyone else.

In our conversations, more accurately the conversations I would eavesdrop on, the kids often shared their dream cars, with many agreeing that a Toyota Camry would be their top choice. Toyota was the dominant car brand in Bangladesh, and the Camry was considered the pinnacle of luxury. At that time, I knew I'd be lucky to even afford an autorickshaw, so I tried to steer clear of those discussions. It's amusing to think about how their faces would change if they knew that, in 2024, the Toyota Camry has become synonymous with taxis and rideshare services like Uber in places like Australia.

Now that I can afford one, I wouldn't want to own a Camry, mainly because I wouldn't want some drunk Australian mistaking my car for an Uber on a Friday night and threatening to give me a one-star rating when I ask them to get out! I think I'd be so offended by the one-star threat that I might actually decide to drop them off at their destination just to preserve that imaginary five-star rating! Social media validation metrics really do have an impact on the way we live!

Anyway, my teenage brain was convinced that flaunting a car was the ultimate way to rack up social points—but that was easier said than done, considering I didn't even have full time access to one! One thing I had going for me was my skill with computers—thanks to all those, ahem, "pirated" video games. Look, I'm not going to justify piracy. But hear me out: if buying something in this day and age doesn't really mean owning it, then pirating for personal use and not profiting off it doesn't count as stealing, right? Besides, academics pirate research papers all the time because huge publishers put knowledge behind paywalls. Education is a basic necessity, yet someone always has to foot the bill. So, why not funnel all the money to the big publishers instead of the academics who actually produce the work? And if you're an academic who believes the knowledge that you produce should be freely accessible, why not pay the publishers yourself to make it "open access" for the readers? Either way, capitalism wins!

Anyway, at school, I overheard the other kids talking about explicit content they couldn't access because of paywalls and restrictions imposed by the government. Label sexual activities as taboo, restrict access to online content, and then hold public summits to investigate why sexual crimes are on the rise—welcome to South Asia!

Though it was an awkward subject, I saw it as an opportunity to connect. Once I set up my broadband connection, I started obtaining this content via "alternative" sources. It wasn't long before I became the guy with access to what no one else could get. I suppose I was looking for the validation I never received at home and simply wanted to feel included and heard.

At first, I awkwardly offered to show people what I had at my house—an idea that in hindsight was downright creepy, so it's no surprise they all declined. I soon pivoted to offering the content on USB drives, free of charge, hoping that would win me some social clout. This didn't land me in the popular crowd, but it did earn me the unfortunate title of "Porno King." Not exactly what I had in mind, but hey, at least it replaced my previous nickname of "egg head."

Before long, kids I didn't even know started slipping me folded pieces of paper with empty thumb drives inside during lunch. These notes had disturbingly specific requests, some of which I'd never even heard of. I'd search for these obscure terms, often horrified by what I found. After loading up the thumb drives, I'd leave them on my desk, and the anonymous requester would pick them up the next day. I made a point of trying not to look them in the eye—I didn't want to associate their faces with the bizarre things they were into.

I'd be lying if I said I didn't enjoy some of the things I downloaded, but after a while, my computer hard drive of one whole terabyte was nearly full. For context, that was a lot of high-definition content in those days. Nida and I attended the same school, and she was often embarrassed when her guy friends approached her with requests to "put in a good word" for them to the King. They wanted her to persuade me, her younger brother, to move their "requests" up in the queue. Yes, I had a massive backlog! Handing everything out for free wasn't sustainable, and to make matters worse, I wasn't gaining any new friends from it either. The whole thing started to feel absurd. I wasn't getting any validation in return, only more perverse requests. So, after a few months, I decided to quit, but the nickname "Porno King" stuck. Two of my closest friends still joke about my days as a "bootlegger" to this day!

One afternoon, Nida called me into her room. "Look at this," she said, showing me a social media message on her phone with a display picture of a guy reading a book.

"Who is that?" I asked.

Nida chuckled, "Definitely someone who does *not* read books but wants to look smart in front of others."

She explained she'd briefly met the guy somewhere, and he had followed up with a message. It was cheesy, but sweet enough to pique her interest. The guy had the "hook" that my story apparently lacks, or so the publishers keep telling me. However, Nida was uncertain about what to do.

"What should I do?" she asked.

I saw an opportunity. "Why not meet him? Tell him your brother's coming along to scope him out. We can meet at KFC!"

She saw through my plan and smirked. Nonetheless, she responded to the guy, "Hi, my brother insists on a free meal. Maybe we can get to know each other while he munches on KFC!"

We both half-expected the guy to ghost her after that, but to our surprise, he laughed and agreed. Chivalry is not dead, yet!

We took the car to meet with him although Nida told father that she was going to the tutor's and I was tagging along for some reason; He didn't bother questioning her since she was taking me, what's the worst that she could do?

She would conveniently have the car parked near her tutor's house while she snuck about doing things on foot or via rickshaw. This was a common sight in Dhaka at the time where girls would sneak out from under their overprotective parents' watch to make bad decisions. To that extent, I think overprotective Asian parents are roughly the Western equivalent of alcohol at a girls' night out!

As we approached her tutor's house, she jumped out of the car and yanked me out by the hand. Chacha and Mizan knew their roles well; they maneuvered the car around the corner to park it. Their routine involved Mizan dozing off in the car while Chacha stood guard in front of the building, waiting for my sister. Truth be told, they both often napped in the parking lot! We crossed the road and took a hooded rickshaw as we whizzed past Mizan and Chacha, who were reclining their car seats to prepare for their routine nap and we were heading off for free chicken!

The guy she met was Kaushal—an average-height, well-groomed guy with a deep voice and a wealth of travel experiences. When we finally met Kaushal, Nida wasted no time laying out her plans like she was starting a PowerPoint presentation. "Just so we're clear," she began,

"I'm not looking for anything long-term right now." Kaushal blinked, looking like he'd walked into an ambush.

She continued, with a tone of awkwardness only Nida could pull off. "First of all, our father might beat the living daylights out of you if he so much as suspects you're thinking about touching me. Secondly, I've got responsibilities—like looking after this chicken-hungry gremlin," she gestured toward me with the grace of someone presenting evidence in court.

To his credit, he accepted Nida's antics and said he wasn't looking to rush into anything long-term but was open to keeping in touch and seeing where things went. It seemed reasonable, but I still thought, "*This won't last!*"

As awkward as that date was, the chicken was good, so no complaints.

When we arrived home and were waiting for the elevator in our apartment parking, I noticed a pale young man making his way down the stairs. He wore a flashy neon-green shirt paired with ripped jeans, the brand name plastered conspicuously down the sides. While his outfit was clearly expensive, it struck me as gaudy and tasteless—though perhaps that was just my personal bias. His white sneakers, emblazoned with logos from all the big shoe companies, were an obvious knockoff, the kind you'd find from a street vendor. His hair was brushed to the side and glistened from an excessive use of hair gel, while his eyes had a slight redness that suggested he might have been up to no good. He walked with a sly smile, folding some bills into his front pocket as he approached. As comical as his outfit was, there was an undeniable air about him that seemed out of place, despite his symmetrical, well-contoured features and the sharp, confident line of his jaw. It was as if his appearance, polished and striking, didn't quite match the awkwardness of his presence. I stared at him as he looked familiar, and he glanced back at me for a moment before quickly turning his gaze away and continuing on his way out of the building. I was deeply disturbed by his brief presence, but as he vanished from view, I turned my focus back to Nida, momentarily forgetting the encounter.

Upon entering our apartment, we found our father sitting at the dining table, staring at the door with a cold gaze. My sister, refusing to acknowledge his presence, walked straight to her room. She probably did that to avoid having to answer the question, "where were you?" I clearly did not get the memo, and I greeted our father. When I turned to head to my own room, he suddenly called out, "Wait!"

I turned around, asking, "Yes, sir?"

"Did something happen?" he inquired.

I replied, "No, sir," and he gestured for me to carry on with a flick of his hand. I walked into my room, relieved and ready to catch up on my assignments.

As I was finishing up some school assignments, I heard footsteps in the kitchen and the sounds of doors opening and closing. That didn't seem to come from the main apartment door, so I figured it was Nida, likely up for a late-night snack. She often snuck around to talk to boys only after our father had fallen asleep.

I stayed quiet, but then I heard footsteps approaching my bedroom door. The light from my room bled under the door, casting a faint glow in the pitch darkness outside. Although I suspected it was my sister, I didn't want to entertain her at 1:00 am. with yet another random request about her dating life. I ignored the footsteps, clearly hearing them circle my room. *She's going to wake Chacha,* I thought, who was probably asleep on the bed next to my door.

Then, suddenly, I heard a wail from the other side—an echoing cry that felt eerily supernatural. I wanted no part of that, especially knowing that there were more people in the house now than during the last break-in. I jumped out of bed and flung open the door. The light from my room spilled out just enough for me to see Chacha asleep, possibly under the influence of Gul, blissfully unaware of the disturbance. The darkness cloaked everything else, as the windows failed to reflect any moonlight into the house, and my eyes struggled to adjust.

I heard bare footsteps darting back toward the kitchen. Too tired to investigate further and worn out from a long day, I closed my door and turned off the light, deciding to go back to bed. I chose not to follow up on that.

The next morning, as I got ready for school, I wandered into the kitchen and noticed Shahana wasn't in her usual routine. I called out her name but received no response. After several attempts, she finally emerged from her quarters behind the kitchen, flustered and pale, clearly scared and fidgety. "Are you alright?" I asked, concerned about her unusual demeanour.

"Yes, sir," she replied quickly, setting some food on the table before retreating back to her tiny quarters behind the kitchen.

Nida joined me at the table, and I asked, "Is everything okay with Shahana? She looks really off."

Nida seemed unsure about how to respond, "Finish your meal and go to school."

At that moment, I felt mature enough to recognise when my questions were being brushed aside and knew not to pry further. I decided to change the subject. "Please remember that I have an invitation to a classmate's house this evening. I had finally been invited to a social event. Sure, being known as the infamous "porno king" wasn't exactly flattering, but for someone who barely had any friends, the thought of being around people—of maybe making some actual connections—was thrilling.

It had taken an entire week of convincing my father for him to suggest, "Talk to your sister, and if she's back home by then, take Chacha and the car with you and be back by 9:00 pm!" That was all I could think about, and I made a point to remind Nida every morning until the day finally arrived—today.

Nida understood how important the day was for me and assured me she would do her best to return on time. That afternoon, I rushed home from school, excitement bubbling within me. I quickly scarfed down lunch and dashed to my room to get ready. As I emerged, I noticed my plate still sitting on the table, untouched by Shahana, which was unusual. Dismissing it, I took my plate to the kitchen, washed it, and dried it before settling down on the living room sofa, positioned right by the dining room, where I could keep an eye on the main door.

Hours ticked by, and I tried calling Nida, but she didn't pick up. I then called Chacha, who confirmed she was in class, providing little solace since I was well aware of her actual whereabouts.

My father eventually emerged, noticing me nervously wiggling my legs on the sofa. He chuckled, "Nida isn't back yet?"

"No, not yet. Could you please call her and ask her to come back quickly?" I pleaded.

He grinned knowingly. "She's at the tutor's, right? I am not getting in the way of her education!"

"Yeah," I replied, feigning nonchalance.

In truth, I knew exactly where she was—out on a date with Kaushal. Chacha was conveniently "parked" at the tutor's house to keep up appearances. But she had promised me she'd be back in time for my event. Chacha and the car were just sitting there for nothing!

"Then could you at least ask Mizan and Chacha to drop me off at my friend's place in the meantime and then go back to pick her up when she's done?" I suggested, my anxiety growing. The place wasn't far, and I could've easily snuck out and hopped on a rickshaw, but no, I had to roll up in a car, flashing wealth I didn't actually have—like a wannabe rapper from a trailer park rocking Air Jordans but too cheap to even consider a dentist! Go big or *stay* home!

I could see the irritation in my father's eyes as he replied, "I told you that you can only go if Chacha stays with you the entire time you are there."

Frustration washed over me as I tried to reason with him, but he silenced me with a sharp tone.

"You're being unreasonable! This is the first time I've been invited anywhere, and you're favouring Nida, who lies to you about her classes and sneaks off to be with her friends!" The moment the words left my mouth, I knew I couldn't take them back. While this kind of teenage rebellion was nothing new for parents, I watched as his expression darkened.

He slowly walked to his room, closing the door behind him, and I could hear him calling my sister. She knew better than to ignore his call. Soon, I heard him yelling at her, demanding she return home immediately. True to his word, she arrived within the hour, but it was already 8:00 pm, far too late for me to attend the party. My heart sank—my first chance at making friends outside of school ruined by Nida's carelessness.

As the main door opened, Nida walked in with a slow, heavy gait, clearly shaken. My father emerged, berating her, asserting that he knew exactly what she had been up to. At first, my sister played innocent, but the realisation that there was no escaping the situation set in. She attempted to ignore him and walk straight into her room, but my father followed her, his angry words echoing as he slammed the door behind him. By that point, they were too far away for me to hear the details, but I couldn't help but feel a sense of justice for what she had done to me.

The next morning, Shahana was noticeably more shaken, her once cheerful demeanour was now dull and completely tinged with sadness. She barely acknowledged me, retreating to her room as soon as she finished her tasks. As I sat down for breakfast before school, Nida emerged, her eyes swollen from crying throughout the night and her cheek swollen and bruised. She took her usual spot at the dining table, and the obnoxious teenager in me couldn't resist the urge to gloat.

"This is what you get for what you did yesterday!" I taunted.

She looked at me blankly and asked, "You told him?"

"Yes!" I replied, half-expecting her to explode in rage. Instead, she responded in a soft, defeated tone, "You shouldn't have." Without touching her food, she stood up and returned to her room, abandoning her original plans for the entire day.

I hadn't anticipated the cascade of events I had unwittingly set in motion the day before, and things quickly began to spiral out of control. When I returned home from school, my father was still there, and he insisted that all three of us have lunch together. Nida sat quietly, and I noticed that my father seemed unusually sympathetic toward her, a stark contrast to his demeanour the day before. He reached out to hold her shoulder, but as his hand approached, she flinched, and he immediately withdrew, resuming his meal in silence.

In an ill-timed moment of impulse, I asked, "Since she's not going anywhere, could I take the car to a friend's house after school?" My real intention was to deliver bootlegged goods to a girl I barely knew, hoping to muster up the courage for two minutes of awkward conversation in her driveway before she inevitably turned and walked away, just like every other one of my so-called "clients." It was innocent enough, albeit childish and undeniably immature.

What I didn't expect was my father's sudden shift. It was as if something inside him snapped. His tremors intensified, and he sneered, making that squeaking sound with his lips. His voice turned cold and dark as he said, "I told you once; I will tell you again! The car belongs to your sister because she chose me in court. It is her 'generosity' that allows you to ride in a car at all, or to enjoy any semblance of comfort in this household after what you did to me!"

Terror gripped me as I realised that he was on the verge of exploding. My heart raced, and I could see him rising from his seat, the tension palpable in the air.

"If it were up to me—"

Before he could finish, Nida, who had been silent until now, inter-jected, "Please don't talk to him like that!" Her voice rang out, desper-ate and shaky, as if she was trying to divert his fury toward herself. In a display of her own fear, she pulled back her chair and gripped the table-cloth over her face, squinting her eyes as if hoping to shield herself from him.

My father fixed his gaze on her, his voice dripping with menace as he asked, "What did you say to me?" In an instant, he seized her by the back of her neck, and I sat frozen in my seat, paralysed by a mix of fear and disbelief.

It was as if a primal instinct kicked in within her. She shoved his hand away and screamed, "He did not choose you; I did! You have no right to take your frustration out on him!" In a violent flash, he grasped a fistful of her wavy hair and slammed her face onto the table. Plates clattered and food flew, the room erupting into chaos.

My heart raced as I met his eyes—dark, filled with a terrifying rage. He bellowed at her to shut up. Stronger than her, he pinned her down, and despite her struggling, she couldn't break free until he let her go. Yet, instead of giving up and retreating, she mustered all her strength and pushed against him, futilely attempting to fight back. She screamed incoherently, her voice a mix of anger and desperation, but he stood there, unyielding and silent with his head tremor evident now, absorbing her blows with an unsettling calmness, waiting for her to tire.

When her energy waned, he grabbed her by the throat, lifting her off the ground and flinging her toward the living room, closer to my room. She crashed to the floor, her small frame barely absorbing the im-pact, and I felt a wave of panic wash over me. I was thrust back to the horrifying memory of the day he had done the same to my mother be-fore beating her with his belt. This time, Nida was smaller, more fragile, and he tossed her around as if she were a ragdoll, landing blows with the back of his hand. One strike landed behind her ear, and she cried out, clutching her head.

She didn't give up, rising again, but each time she was met with a brutal shove that sent her crashing back down. Her incoherent screams filled the room, while I remained paralysed at the dining table, unable to move or intervene. I had a choice to make, and I chose to do nothing! He kicked her while she was down, then yanked her up again by the back of her neck, hurling her toward Chacha's bed. She stumbled, her knee colliding with the short bedpost with a dull thud that threw her completely off balance. She collapsed onto the bed with a sickening crack, her body folding awkwardly. Her head and upper body slid off the edge, landing face down on the floor, while the rest of her remained draped limply across the bed.

The sound of that crack froze my father in his tracks. He stopped, his rage dissipating as suddenly as it had flared. Breathing heavily, he stood there, surveying the wreckage he had caused with cold, detached eyes. Not a flicker of emotion crossed his face. After a long, suffocating pause, he turned and walked out of the room without a word, passing by Shahana who stood still in the kitchen, her eyes empty, her expression as lifeless as Nida's, who now lay motionless in front of me.

Chapter 6. The help

For what felt like an eternity, I remained frozen, my gaze locked on Nida, searching for even the slightest movement. Slowly, I noticed her body shaking with sobs. It was then that something shifted inside me. I crawled to her side as she wept, and all I could manage to whisper was, "I'm sorry." She reached for my hand, but her grip was weak, a feeble echo of the times she'd yanked me away with that same motion. This time, she couldn't even hold on properly.

I helped her up, and we settled onto Chacha's bed. "Are you alright? How's your knee?" I asked, the most obvious question I could think of.

"It's nothing that won't heal. I don't think anything's broken," she replied. Her voice was tinged with fatigue. But before she could say more, her gaze shifted upward, and her expression fell silent. I followed her eyes and saw our father, impeccably dressed in his crisp formal attire, walking out of the house.

Words failed me, and I found myself staring at her, caught in a web of uncertainty. She barely met my gaze before murmuring, "You shouldn't have told him." A harrowing realisation gripped me—she had likely endured a storm of rage the night before.

Frozen in place, I continued to watch her until she finally broke the silence. "Don't worry; this isn't the first time. Likely won't be the last time either."

"Why?" I asked, guilt and desperation creeping into my voice.

"Because I don't have anyone else. I chose to stay with him when my mother wanted to leave." Her words felt heavy, a confession laden with sorrow rather than a direct answer to my question. She was trapped in this cycle of violence, having accepted it as a grim reality of her existence. "He's not always like this though. He cares for the most part."

She forced a smile, though the swelling and bruises began to mar her facial features. "You know, I can't hear in one of my ears," she said, her voice almost playful, as if she were trying to lighten the mood.

"Is it from the blow today?" I asked, concern knitting my brows.

"No, it's from when I was younger." She paused, her eyes distant.

I was at a loss for words. I sat in silence beside her, wishing she would tell me what to do next. Instead, she rested her head on my shoulder, and I found myself staring at the cracked bedpost wondering what I had done. She was my father's favourite, right? Was this the price that she had to pay?

The most notable change in the next few weeks was my sister bringing home a sick, scruffy rescue puppy she'd found on the side of the road. She named him Timmy. After taking him to get vaccinated and setting up a small playpen in her room, she was completely smitten with him. Unlike our old dog, Sargeant, Timmy was tiny—far too small to be a guard dog or offer any protection against our father.

I understood why people rescue helpless animals, but we weren't equipped to care for a dog at home. I assumed Nida had taken in Timmy as a coping mechanism, a way to preserve her mental sanity. Timmy had a quirky personality. He loved to circle the support pillars in our building, always restless, never staying still. He barked endlessly at anyone who passed by our main door—a classic case of "all bark, no bite."

The real trouble came from Nida's inability to toilet-train him. Timmy had developed the habit of relieving himself on any rice sack lying around, likely a remnant of his days on the streets. My sister tried to make do by allocating empty rice sacks in the corner of her room, but despite her best efforts, he remained untrainable. What started as an adorable, endearing pup eventually turned into a menace. Timmy grew snappier with strangers, barking and nipping at anyone new who came too close.

He soon became a source of tension between us. Nida refused to consider rehoming him, even as he became more difficult to manage. It became especially frustrating for me since Timmy preferred relieving himself near my room, often at my doorstep!

When we all sat at the dinner table—Nida laughed and chatted with my father like their violent encounter had ever happened. It felt surreal, almost like I was in a different reality. What shocked me even more was his acceptance of Timmy, quirks and all. He even made light of the dog's odd behaviour, cracking jokes about Timmy's hyperactivity. Every so often, he would glance at me, searching for validation of his humour, as though my reaction mattered.

By that point, I was so terrified of him that I forced myself to smile whenever his eyes landed on me, hoping it would somehow shield me from whatever darkness lurked beneath the surface.

One afternoon, as I returned home from school, I saw the apartment door partially open and heard Timmy barking from inside Nida's closed room. We would send Timmy into my sister's room and close the door whenever we had visitors.

We have visitors – I thought! Inside, I found my father talking to an old man and two young girls, likely sisters, no older than thirteen. One of the girls had a prominent scar running along her right cheek. The old man was likely their guardian. Their guardian was pleading with my father, "Please, sir, they can learn to work around the house. You can pay them whatever you think is appropriate, just give them a roof over their heads. We are no longer able to support them." As I stepped out of the lift and walked closer to the door, I saw a fifth person standing with them.

I stood and watched. My father, acknowledged the guardian's desperation with a strange empathetic expression, agreed, and turned to hand some money to the fifth person in the room whom he referred to as Ranjan—the same man in the tastelessly expensive clothes I'd seen leaving the building the other night as Nida and I were waiting for the lift. That name rang a bell! He provided my father with the hired help when *Dadu* was ill. Ranjan took the money, handing a share to the old man before leading him away. He passed by me without even acknowledging my presence, as if I were invisible, and took the stairs down instead of the lift just like last time.

My father then walked the two girls to the small, cramped live-in maid's quarters. "This is where you'll stay, once Shahana leaves" he said flatly. "If it gets too warm in here, you can always sleep on the floor in the dining room after dinner. Don't worry, the dog gets used to new faces very soon and spends the night in my daughter's rooms."

I stood by the doorway, watching. As my father calmly walked into his room, he paused without turning, only to instruct me to lock the main door on my way in. Seeing the two young girls, barely a year younger than I was, didn't immediately seem bad. "*At least we were able to help a few people in need. Shame Shahana has to leave though.*" I thought.

I suppose after seeing so much, you eventually become desensitised to the darker aspects of life. In our community, poverty was so widespread that it was common for children from poor rural families to work—either in factories or as live-in maids for wealthier families in the cities. Often, the parents would lie about the children's age to get them hired, though it was usually obvious they were younger than they claimed.

That evening, when Nida came home, she followed her usual routine—coming straight into my room to check on me before heading to hers to check on Timmy. She walked in with her usual goofy tone, asking, "What's uuuup?"

I was playing on my computer but paused the game and turned to her as she stood at the door to tell her the news. "Shahana left, but we have new maids," I said, emphasising the plural. "They're my age!" I added, expecting her to be intrigued. But instead, I watched her face drain of colour. She didn't say a word and left my room without a reaction, leaving the door ajar.

Curious, I watched her from my doorway as she made her way to the kitchen. She stood there, just looking as the sisters were preparing dinner, as if trying to process something or verify what I had told her. After a long moment, she turned and walked toward our father's room. He was home, and as soon as she entered, I sensed something was off.

By then, I had picked up the kind of habit every melodramatic soap opera housewife would flaunt—eavesdropping. Maybe it was my way of staying alert, a subconscious defence mechanism. Quietly, I slipped out of my room and inched toward my father's door. I could hear the tension in their voices before I even got close. It wasn't just an argument this time; her tone had shifted—almost pleading.

As I approached the door, I heard her say, "Please, let them go. Not them! Please!"

The panic in her voice froze me in place, and in an instant, the door handle began to turn. Terrified of being caught, I bolted into Nida's room right next door, my heart pounding as I tried to make sense of what I had just heard. Timmy noted I walked into her room and came to me looking up inquisitively.

My father walked out of the room, saying coldly, "Fine, I'll let them go. I'll ask Ranjan to find us someone else"

He dialled Ranjan and instructed him to notify the girls' guardian to come and take them home. The girls needed this job desperately, and their family relied on the income. The girls pleaded to stay, even breaking down in tears, fearing they'd return to poverty and hunger. Their desperation was heartbreaking, but my sister, despite understanding their plight, stood firm in her decision. She insisted on removing them, convinced that something terrible was bound to happen if they stayed. She wasn't cruel—she was trying to protect them from a situation she knew all too well, one that no amount of money could justify to her.

People will always have opinions, and they'll judge you for how you respond, without fully understanding the depth of your reasoning. It's easy for others to jump to conclusions, to say what *they* would have done without seeing the full picture. At the time, while I did not fully understand her reasoning at the time, I supported her in her decision. There isn't going to be a grand reveal, so formulate your own opinions of the situation.

The two girls stayed with us for no more than a week before they were taken away. During that time, just as my father had predicted, the live-in quarters were too cramped for two people, so they slept on the dining room floor. Innocent and inseparable, the sisters couldn't sleep without each other.

I began hearing footsteps late at night—just like the ones I'd heard when Shahana stayed with us. They came around 1:00 am. like clockwork, and whenever I was awake, I'd hear them without fail. At first, I always assumed the later footsteps belonged to Timmy, somehow sneaking out of Nida's room for a quiet midnight stroll. But the steps never quite sounded like paws—they were too heavy. Tonight, though, the steps were different: lighter, quicker, almost delicate. This time, there were also several footsteps, and some were unmistakably the soft, rapid taps of a dog's paws. I knew exactly who it was—and who was following her.

Determined to catch them, I opened my door and, instead of squinting into the darkness like before, I marched straight to the switchboard and flicked the lights on. Just as I suspected, I saw Nida standing at the corner of the dining room, with Timmy by her side, his tiny tail wagging excitedly, clearly thrilled about his late-night escapade. But Nida wasn't there for a stroll; she was standing still, her eyes fixed on the two girls asleep on the floor, completely unfazed by the sudden brightness flooding the room.

"What are you doing?" I asked, confused by the way she stood so eerily still.

She barely acknowledged me, her gaze locked on the sleeping girls. "Turn off the lights and go to bed," she muttered, her voice sharp but distant.

She was standing guard, protecting them from something lurking in the shadows that only she could see. I stood there for a moment, unsure of what to say or do, I said "I'm standing with you". She looked at me, sighed and then turned around and made her way back to her room. Timmy followed her, wagging his tail as he padded behind her. I quietly turned off the lights and went back to my own room.

At school, I often found myself sitting alone at lunch. One afternoon, the school's most notorious "delinquent" approached and sat next to me. There were heaps of rumours that he was "a murderer who escaped trial." I had seen him around a few times but had never spoken to him before. Parents frequently warned their kids to steer clear of him, claiming he was up to no good and suggesting he was involved with "illicit" activities such as dealing drugs and alcohol. They also claimed his friends were nothing but drug dealers and goons who hated on honest, hardworking politicians. That was enough to make me dismiss the rumours—I mean, come on, when was the last time you saw an honest politician? Suffice to say his reputation wasn't excellent!

Before we proceed, let me make one thing exceptionally clear: this isn't the start of some clichéd love story between a bad boy and an awkward nerd, like the kind flooding the self-published romantic novel scene. While I have no issues with anyone's sexual orientation—as long as they don't feel the need to lecture me on how to stay organised just because they think being queer makes them an expert—that's simply not the story I'm here to tell.

He stood in front of me for a moment, as if gathering the courage to say something. Then he pulled out a small notebook, scribbled his phone number on a piece of paper, ripped it out, and handed it to me. "We play football at the community field. You should come by sometime," he said casually.

In the early 2010s, most schools in Bangladesh had strict no-electronics policies, which meant cell phones were banned. If you were caught with one, your parents would be called. But I didn't care much about that. I knew who he was; we just hadn't interacted one-on-one before. As I held the slip of paper, a group of kids from another table saw the interaction and approached me after he left. "He's trouble. Stay away from him," they warned me. I couldn't help but think: I spent so long wanting to talk to people, but no one ever bothered to listen. Now, someone finally wants to engage, and suddenly, everyone's here to tell me how wrong this is. It's like human nature thrives on correcting others but not actually helping them!

Maybe I should have listened. But by that point, the part of me that craved validation and acceptance was long gone. I had lost interest in making friends; all I wanted was some peace. Funny how you often get what you stop wanting. His invitation felt sincere, unlike the others who had pretended to be my friends only to abandon me when they realised I wasn't as wealthy as I had claimed, or kept me around for their own amusement, taking advantage of my naivety.

My instincts didn't scream that this fellow was trouble. Maybe he'd just noticed I was always alone and wanted to help or wanted to sell me drugs in which case I could always say "no!"— That's what Western education teaches you, right? Consent matters, always! If you're selling drugs, ask permission first! And in the middle of some naughty foreplay, ready to strip your partner's knickers off? Stop everything, kill the mood, and then ask for permission!

So, despite the warnings, I called him that afternoon. "Hey, can I come over to play today? What time's the match?" I asked. There was a pause before he replied, "Sure, let me arrange it," and hung up.

It felt a bit odd that he had to "arrange" it, but my gut didn't say anything was wrong. Honestly, my instincts were never that great, but I figured I'd give it a shot.

Later, he texted me: "Be there at 4:30 pm."

I grabbed my worn-out sneakers and headed out. As I stepped outside, Mizan pulled up in our Toyota Saloon. Nida likely returned from her tutor's place. She got out of the car and offered, "You can take the car to wherever you're going."

I paused. "It's okay, I'm not going far," I said, knowing that showing off wealth I didn't have wasn't worth it. What's the worst that could happen? Get mugged like Nida did?

For the first time, I wasn't worried about appearances. My sneakers were worn, my phone was outdated, and I barely had enough money for a rickshaw ride. After what felt like a long pause, I said, "I'm good. Mizan can go home; he deserves a rest." I hailed a rickshaw and headed to the meeting spot.

For once, it felt liberating not to be consumed by the need to flaunt wealth I didn't possess.

At the field, I sat in the corner when a group of three boys approached—kids I'd seen at school but never really spoke to. They had a reputation as "delinquents on the verge of incarceration!" They stood in front of me and, as if we were complete strangers, introduced themselves one by one, first Shiro, then Rajesh. The last person to introduce himself was also the guy who invited me over. "I'm Sufi Hamza," he said with a grin. Picking up on the playful tone, I introduced myself too. Sufi was a tall, slender guy with an awkward crew cut and a boxy smile that always made him seem like he had no clue what he was doing. His signature look was socks with sandals, baggy old jeans, and a round t-shirt perpetually adorned with dirt and food stains—no matter where he went. Shiro, on the other hand, was athletic and exuded a stereotypical "bad boy" vibe that made him a magnet for the girls at school. He sported the cliched black leather jacket, aviator sunglasses, and a cigarette—though I was convinced he only lit them up to look cool, never actually taking a proper drag. Then there was Rajesh, the short, stubby one with impressively long, silky hair. He was the most normal of the trio, primarily because he was probably the only kid at school who never made a porno request to me. They were all much older than me.

Sufi cursed a lot. For the sake of keeping this story clean, I'll filter out most of that. "I was waiting on a few other people I know who just didn't show up," he said, as the others burst into laughter. Shiro, teased him, "You were always good for nothing!"

After waiting around for about thirty minutes, Sufi threw his hands up in mock frustration. "I got stood up!" Then, turning to me, he added with a smirk, "I know a guy who knows a guy who said some interesting things about your stash," referring to my days of distributing explicit content. "Let's go to your place, and you can show us what you've been up to!"

"I don't do that anymore," I said quickly, but Sufi just laughed. "I'm sure we can find something else to do!"

As Sufi and Shiro started heading out of the field, they turned to Rajesh, and Sufi asked, "Well, are you going to drive us there or what?". Rajesh laughed and said, "As long as nobody records me while you're browsing through that stuff! I don't want to be associated with porn"

Sufi merely smirked.

Oddly enough, the interaction didn't feel intimidating. It felt fun. I led them to my place, and as soon as we stepped out of the elevator and reached my door, Timmy, our tiny dog, started barking. All three boys bolted toward the stairs, with Sufi yelling, "We didn't know you had a dog! How big is it?"

I couldn't help but laugh. "Timmy's tiny, he just barks a lot." And in my head, I thought, "*What kind of hooligans are these guys, scared of a little barking?*"

When Chacha opened the door, I awkwardly blurted, "Look, I don't have any money at home. We're not that rich... well, at least I'm not." They looked confused, so I shut up before I embarrassed myself further. As they entered, they saw Timmy barking away, held on a leash by the maid.

Rajesh quickly asked, "Which way's your room?" I pointed them in the right direction, and without hesitation, the three of them ran straight in, not even stopping to look around. It was the first time I had friends over, and I didn't even have to put on a show.

In my room, they were surprisingly impressed by my modest 19-inch monitor next to my bed. Shiro joked, "This would make a great place for a movie night!"

Unsure if he was serious, I asked, "What do you have in mind?"

Rajesh chimed in, "We could go to the DVD store nearby and grab a movie—and maybe some dinner too."

"I don't have enough for that," I said quietly. "You guys go ahead." My father still gave me just enough to make it the entire month and not a penny more.

They exchanged glances, went quiet for a second, and then said, "Okay," before quickly leaving, just like they'd run from Timmy. I knew they weren't coming back, but that was alright. For once, I'd had a good time.

Two hours had passed while I was working on my assignments when the doorbell rang again. Chacha took Timmy on his leash, and opened the door. I heard familiar voices—it was Rajesh, Shiro, and Sufi. Respectfully, they asked, "Sir, which way is your kitchen?"

Curious, I opened my door just in time to see them rushing into the kitchen, each carrying bags full of groceries. Confused, I ran after them, "What are you guys doing?"

Sufi grinned. "We didn't feel like eating out, so we thought we'd whip something up. Is it cool if we use your kitchen?"

I realised they were trying to include me, so I played along, watching as Chacha took Timmy to Nida's room. My sister became curious about the commotion, came out to meet the boys. They greeted her with respect, far from the ill-mannered delinquents I'd been warned about.

In the kitchen, we tried cooking something together, none of us having a clue what we were doing. The result? A disaster. The noodles were so burnt and melted that we had to toss the whole thing out. Rajesh looked at Sufi, "Order some chicken, Sufi. This noodle mess is your fault!"

Knowing how expensive a bucket of fried chicken would be, I told them not to bother. But Sufi had already made the call.

Shiro whispered, "Don't worry, Sufi's got money." Sufi, overhearing, turned around and shouted, "Don't put ideas into his head! I'm broke. I'll have to trade his dog for that chicken!"

We all burst out laughing. Soon enough, the doorbell rang, and a delivery boy arrived with a large bucket of chicken. I went to take the bucket, but before I could even get the receipt, Sufi ran over, grabbed it, and paid out of his own pocket. I felt like the guest in my own house, unable to afford the meal, but they never made me feel that way.

The four of us sat in front of my modest 19-inch screen, eating chicken and watching a movie they'd brought over. As I sat there, I couldn't shake a feeling of uncertainty. What's their angle? Why would they hang out with someone like me? I couldn't hold it in any longer. I paused the movie and asked, "What's the deal? People like you don't hang out with people like me."

Sufi laughed, "We had a good time. Does it really matter where or with whom?"

Shiro, noticing my unease, asked, "What do you mean 'people like you'?"

Naïve as I was, I blurted out everything I'd heard at school and from parents about them—the rumours, the gossip. When I finished, they looked at each other and burst into laughter.

Rajesh spoke up first. "I knew we'd be labelled drug dealers and murderers. I'm surprised we weren't called human traffickers too!"

Confused, I asked, "What do you mean?"

Rajesh explained, "Sufi liked this girl, and she had a friend who wanted to try alcohol and weed."

Shiro jumped in, "This friend weighed over 120 kilos! That's important!"

Sufi grinned, "So I knew a guy who knew a guy who sold alcohol to underaged kids, and I knew another guy with a cousin who sold weed."

Rajesh rolled his eyes at Sufi and continued, "When the girl asked Sufi to get her friend some booze and weed, he went and got it. Didn't even tell us. Puppy love."

"Shut up, Rajesh!" Sufi laughed. "Just tell him the story."

Rajesh went on, "So Sufi shows up at the girl's place with weed and alcohol in his backpack. The girl tells him to bring it up to the roof, and the three of them drink and smoke. But the big girl drinks half the bottle!"

Shiro added, "Yeah, and then she passed out!"

Rajesh continued, "Next thing we know, Sufi's calling us, saying, 'I need help moving a body!' We thought he'd finally gone and done it this time!"

Shiro, barely able to contain his laughter, chimed in, "So we go to the roof, and the girl's friend is freaking out, saying she can't be caught, and runs off, leaving us with a passed-out whale!"

Sufi laughed, "Shiro, be respectful!"

Rajesh finished the story, "We didn't know what to do, so Sufi grabs her legs, I grab her arms, and we carry her down to my car, with Shiro trailing behind with the empty bottle of vodka. Just as we're loading her into the car, some parents drive by and see us putting an unconscious girl into the backseat while Shiro's hunting for a recycling bin to ditch the bottle!"

Shiro laughed, "And that's how the rumours started that now we entered the trade of human trafficking too!"

"The funniest part," Rajesh said, "was that she woke up right after we put her in the car. Could've saved us a lot of trouble if she'd woken up fifteen minutes earlier!"

I hadn't laughed that hard in ages. When I finally caught my breath, I asked, "Weren't the police involved?"

Sufi grinned, "For what? She walked away fine, the bottle was recycled, and all the weed was in the whale!"

Shiro joked again, "Sufi, be respectful!"

And just like that, we became friends. From that day on, they stuck around, and I didn't mind being labelled part of "the wrong crowd" because, honestly, I enjoyed their company. People would still associate them with gangs or trouble, but what they didn't realise was that these "hooligans" taught me another life lesson: people will always judge.

It's important to form your own judgment based on your personal experiences with someone, rather than relying on hearsay or assumptions. As the saying goes, "Don't judge a book by its cover," but even more fitting is Suzanne Massie's iconic phrase: "Trust, but verify." My friends helped me mature enough to understand that while feedback is valuable, the final decision should always come from what I believe is right. Seeking validation from others often leads nowhere—ten different people will have ten different opinions. Human nature is judgmental, sometimes even biased, and chasing approval can leave you feeling lost.

So, were these three innocent? Of course not: But then, no one is! In just one year, my new friends introduced me to everything I'd been sheltered from. We started hanging out at gaming bars and playing football regularly, which introduced me to a wide range of people, some of whom met tragic ends due to drug abuse. One of the queer boys we hung out with was allegedly sexually assaulted and killed by an older foreign coach. The boy's body was later discovered in a lake, and the coach was deported—A slap on the wrist, if you ask me. Shortly after, Sufi convinced us to enrol in Karate, supposedly so we could defend ourselves if "someone came after our anuses," as Sufi put it. That didn't last long as our karate instructor retired after taking a tumble from a tree outside a girls' dormitory while spying on a girl in the shower.

Sufi had barely learnt how to drive and was taking turns with Rajesh as we travelled halfway across the country with them on road trips.

We narrowly escaped a fatal car crash with Sufi behind the wheels at the grand junction of Dhaka-Sylhet Highway. I saw the red-light district at night, ventured into pubs and clubs, and met people who later turned out to be drug dealers. One of the people we hung out with, the daughter of a hotelier, sold methamphetamine to classmates during their stay at her own family hotel, charging them hotel fees to fund her entire operation; This is called "double dipping" in finance and tax! I watched weed and meth transform the brightest athletes into gaunt shadows of themselves, eventually dropping out of teams because the drugs they once used to boost stamina became the very thing that drained it. I was even dragged into hosting one of the largest underground parties in the city at the time!

But did that mean Sufi, Shiro, and Rajesh were bad human beings? That is subjective. Their social circle might have been questionable, but in my opinion, they weren't. They never drank or indulged in any of the vices themselves, nor did they encourage me or anyone else to do so. When I once admitted how sheltered I had been, Sufi responded, "The more of the world you see, the better equipped you'll be to make your own decisions and avoid ignorance. Choices matter, you know!"

Looking back now, I fully agree with that philosophy. Sheltering someone may protect them for a time, but it leaves them vulnerable to far greater dangers later. Life is about experience—about seeing the world firsthand so you can navigate it wisely. In that sense, while I was exposed to everything all at once, I've come to believe that a controlled level of exposure to life's vices is crucial when paired with showing kids the real consequences under proper supervision. How a parent chooses to approach this is the challenge and will remain at the discretion of the individual's parenting style. It's something our Asian parents often failed to grasp while I was growing up. Sheltering alone isn't enough; sometimes, seeing the reality is the best teacher.

Am I still part of that life? No. Would I ever be tempted to return to it? Absolutely not. I've already been there and seen, up close, the consequences people face when they get too deep. That experience was enough for me to know that it's not a path I want to walk again. It shaped my perspective, not by enticing me, but by teaching me what to avoid.

During that time, Sufi wanted me to tutor him so he could improve his education, claiming he wanted to make something of himself. At first, I wasn't sure if he was serious, but he showed up for our study sessions whenever I asked, putting in genuine effort—even though he struggled with concepts that seemed easy to me. His repeated failures in school years only made things harder, contrary to the common Bangladeshi belief at the time that repeating a grade automatically gives someone a better chance. If the reasons behind their failure aren't addressed, repeating the year changes nothing. I quickly realised his foundation was weak, so I started with the basics—fifth grade level. There was a sense of satisfaction when he finally began grasping concepts that teachers had previously written him off for. In the process of tutoring Sufi, I found myself genuinely enjoying academics and, surprisingly, improving in my own studies as well.

By that time, I started growing out of my awkward phase. My hair had started growing long enough for me to tie it into a small ponytail as my facial features became more defined. Playing football for the local team helped develop my physique, and as I grew taller, I built a reputation for no longer being the shy kid who could be picked on or mocked. Having the boys back me up in front of bullies helped too. But I started becoming aggressive over little things, either because of testosterone, or perhaps as a way to compensate for all the times I stayed silent when I should have spoken up.

Sufi began spending more time at our place during the day as I helped him with his studies. Despite being a bit rough around the edges, he was surprisingly dedicated—a serious student putting in genuine effort. It was the kind of transformation no one would expect from someone branded as a "delinquent."

Naturally, Mizan couldn't ignore the changes. He noticed Sufi's frequent visits and started hearing whispers from the other chauffeurs at school, all gossiping about Sufi's supposedly shady reputation. Rumours, as usual, travelled faster than facts. He grew concerned and informed my father, unaware of what kind of person my father really was. This didn't sit well with my father, who, though aware that I was growing stronger, underestimated how afraid I still was of him. No matter how strong a front I put on, the years of trauma he had inflicted left permanent scars. He had imposed an 8:00 pm. curfew on me and would often call Chacha to confirm whether I was home when my father was at Pirojpur. It might sound like good parenting until you realise he started snapping if I came home at 7:30, thinking it was much later. He'd often call and scream at me for being out at 11:00 pm. when it was actually just 6:30 pm. I concluded that he often made those calls under the influence of alcohol.

One afternoon, I sprained my leg on the way home from school after falling into one of the hundreds of potholes that corrupt government contractors apparently filled with sponge and a prayer from someone's mother. It cracks under the weight of the first morbidly obese kid who walks over it. I had to visit the emergency department at Kuddus Memorial Hospital. The wait was painfully long, very similar to the queues in Australian hospital emergency wards. Unless you're at death's door, you're in for a marathon. As I sat in the waiting room until 7:00 pm, I resigned myself to the fact that even if I were seen quickly, the trip back home would be another ordeal. Dhaka traffic at that hour was infamous, and I'd likely spend an hour and a half crawling through it.

Knowing my father hadn't been home when I left, I decided to call Chacha and give him a heads-up. "If Father calls, please tell him I'll be late. I'm at the doctor's office," I said casually. To my surprise, Chacha whispered, his tone uneasy. "He's home," he said, sounding almost scared.

I was terrified. I hadn't expected that, and now I had to notify him. Swallowing my fear, I called him, but there was no answer. Knowing he never read text messages, I called a few more times to leave enough evidence that I had made an effort. When I arrived home, it was already 9:00 pm. I limped to the elevator and reached our floor, only to find the door wide open and everyone inside shaken. Chacha wouldn't speak to me, and our maid was crying in the kitchen, plates and objects scattered across the floor as if a fight had broken out. I ran to Nida's room, hoping they were both okay. Opening the door, I found Timmy, our dog, cowering and squeaking, clearly traumatised. Nida lay on the floor bleeding from her mouth. She did not even try to get up. It was a scene I had seen before.

I hurried to her side, helping her to her feet. "Did he take it out on you again?" I asked, already knowing the answer.

Too exhausted to speak, with swollen cheeks and bruised jaws from the assault, she simply nodded.

This time, I didn't freeze—I was furious. While I should have approached the situation with more control, anger overwhelmed me. "I'm going to talk to him," I said, preparing to leave her room.

Before I could go, Nida grabbed my hand, pleading, "He's not himself today. It's not his fault. Please leave it."

Her words didn't calm me. Guilt and rage pushed me forward, my fear of him replaced with boiling hatred. I stormed into his room, entering it for the first time since moving in. We were never allowed to enter his room, but after everything he had done, I wasn't about to let that stop me. The room was sparse—just a queen-sized bed, a wardrobe, and a large metal trunk. The bed was elevated by four metal feet, leaving some clearance beneath it, likely to have tins of biscuits and treats stashed away underneath. The mattress was plain, nothing fancy. The curtains were drawn, and only a single shaded light fixture dimly lit the room. The air reeked of alcohol. A half-empty bottle of whiskey lay on the floor next to the bed, the bottle cap resting on top of the mattress. The bathroom door was closed, and I could hear my father inside, coughing and vomiting.

As I moved closer, I bent down to cap the bottle to prevent it from tipping over. That's when I noticed something sticking out from under the bed—just barely visible. I leaned in, and my father's retching in the bathroom grew louder as I got closer to the floor. Then I saw it—toes sticking out from under the bed.

My heart raced as I dropped to the floor, pressing myself flat against the cold surface. Peering beneath the bed, my breath caught. A pair of half-lidded, glassy eyes stared back at me—intoxicated and unfocused. A young girl lay there, trembling like a leaf caught in a storm. Her lips quivered as she murmured, "Please...sir" but the rest of her words dissolved into an incoherent whisper, swallowed by her fear. I recognised her immediately—it was Shahana. But she had left a year ago!

Chapter 7. Alone

Poverty often drives people to make choices they aren't proud of, and desperation can blur moral boundaries even further. When someone with wealth offers you a way out of your predicament, asking for nothing more than what you already possess, a less educated individual might accept without considering the long-term consequences. Even if they have reservations, family pressure can push them to think about the greater good of their household. As long as the individual claims to be over eighteen years old and signs a legal document in exchange for some money, it all becomes legal.

In Bangladesh, this can be seen as a form of monetary exchange akin to prostitution, which is technically legal. The country is home to Daulatdia, the largest brothel town in the world, but you don't have to go that far to find individuals willing to accept payment for your pleasures. Many maids and domestic workers in Bangladesh come from impoverished backgrounds and are compensated accordingly. Unlike in Australia, where labour laws are strictly enforced, workers in rural areas are often willing to accept any substantial increment to their meagre village wages. This desperation leads them to hand over their passports—and with them, their identities—to overseas syndicates that promise better-paying jobs abroad.

When not sent overseas, these syndicates act as middlemen, connecting poor individuals from remote villages with wealthy families in the city seeking domestic help for minimal pay. The middleman collects a finder's fee from both parties and takes a commission from each salary, ensuring that only a fraction of the earnings makes its way back to the maid's family in the village. Sometimes these middlemen are related by blood to the domestic help they represent.

This issue is not confined to Bangladesh; it occurs worldwide. It represents a form of symbiotic trafficking, where victims retain a degree of autonomy while providing services to those in power. Calling the authorities is not helpful as the victims will hardly ever cooperate. Silence can be bought, and the cost of speaking up is too high! Unfortunately, they are rarely treated well. Although the traditional mindset is gradually fading, giving way to more educated perspectives, the decline in such practices is not happening quickly enough to suggest that they will cease to exist in the coming decades.

That night, as I stared at the motionless figure beneath my father's bed, a grim understanding washed over me. I began to comprehend the events of the last ten years: why so many people had left, and why they had stopped respecting my mother as she endured beatings in front of them. I recognised that this was more than I had ever been prepared to face. In that moment of stark clarity, I took a deep breath to steady myself. Without addressing the disoriented figure under the bed, I quietly stood up, left the room, and made my way to Nida.

Outside, I found her pacing anxiously, her eyes meeting mine with uncertainty. She broke the silence first. "I told you. He just had a little too much to drink. He'll be fine tomorrow."

I quickly interrupted, "Drinking is the least of our concerns. There is a girl under his bed. I think its Shahana, the maid that left a year ago."

Her face went pale, and she could only manage a whisper, "...but he promised he wouldn't."

In that moment, she grabbed my hand, yanking me in a way that felt familiar. Despite being stronger now, I allowed myself to be led, but instead of directing me to our father's room, she took me to my own. She closed the door behind her and began to cry.

I tried to console her, urging her to clarify the situation. "Isn't it time that I know everything?" I asked.

"He promised. He promised he would stop!" she cried, her voice shaking with emotion. We both knew he was the one who had always preached that a promise should never be broken.

After a moment, she recomposed herself, looking me in the eyes. "It's like he doesn't even remember his own promises now. Please let me handle this."

"I should be there..." I started, but she quickly cut me off. "That will only make it worse. Please trust me!"

I was stubborn. "I don't care; I need to—"

"Please, for once, think about me!" she implored, her voice rising. "I have an offer for a university in the UK. He's agreed to pay for the tuition. Can't you see? This is my way out! I can't do anything to ruin this. Please let me have this!" She broke down, tears streaming down her face.

I managed to ask, "You're leaving?"

"Yes," she replied, her voice trembling. "I made him set aside the money for it. I've been doing it for years by telling him all sorts of things. I can't ruin this."

"But you didn't tell me?" I asked, hurt.

"I couldn't take that risk anymore with you!" she shot back, and I realised she had a valid point. I had broken her trust once before, and I couldn't deny that.

Understanding the gravity of the situation, I reluctantly agreed that it would be best for her to handle it.

I listened intently through my door as Nida approached my father's room. She didn't have to go far; he had sobered up just enough to step out for a glass of water. Nida inched closer to him, her voice rising with desperation: "You promised, you promised, YOU PROMISED!" Her tone shifted to a scream, "Get out of here now!" In that moment, something within her shattered, and the tone she used with him would stay in her for years to come. Surprisingly, my father remained silent. I heard his door open and close, signalling that someone had entered just as my sister returned to my room, her eyes glistening with tears.

A moment later, we heard footsteps move towards the apartment's main door, followed by the lift door chiming open and then closing. They were gone.

Nida exited my room and turned to Chacha and asked, "What was he wearing?"

"Crisp clothes and the silver chain," Chacha replied softly almost knowing what he needed to say.

Looking at me, she said, "He's not coming back tonight." A sigh of relief escaped her lips, but I couldn't help but notice the bruises that marred her arms, likely from the altercation that occurred before I arrived.

"I am sure that was Shahana under his bed. What is going on? I thought she left." I asked. Nida responded quietly, "Shahana is probably the daughter of some farmer who fell on hard times again and decided to sell out their own blood in exchange for a saving hand."

I frowned, "And you're okay with him exploiting the weak like that?"

She looked away, her voice soft but firm. "He's all I have. I chose this life." Then, almost to convince herself, she added, "Besides, if he didn't do it, the farmer would have gone to someone else who might have treated the poor girl worse. At least here, I can keep watch and look after them."

I pressed, "How does that really help?"

Nida paused, her expression hardening. "He promised me. He'll tell me when he does something like this, that it'll be consensual, and the girls will be over eighteen. He had always kept his promise until tonight."

I didn't dare ask how many of those promises my father had broken that night.

What she was suggesting sounded like the typical spiel health gurus use to promote wellness pills and probiotics. These products that only serve as placebos, making gurus money off affiliate links. Father got what he wanted, Nida was getting her ticket out, and everyone else in the middle was left getting taken for a ride.

In the coming days, as the tension began to dissipate, Timmy, still traumatised, began to lash out at Nida. The vet had recommended a re-homing program, and reluctantly, she decided to give him away. Mizan handed in his resignation. Chacha grew quieter, clearly upset by everything that had transpired.

Dinner times grew increasingly quiet as Nida planned her departure to the UK.

For international students heading to places like the UK or Australia, demonstrating financial means is a Lieutenant hurdle. My sister had been saving up for years, convincing our father to put money for the cause into their joint account, which he controlled. This was also the account where all the rent from Pirojpur would accumulate that Nida would use to pay our own rent in Uttara when the Lieutenant was away.

One morning during breakfast, our father brought up an investment idea. Nida immediately sensed trouble.

"How much, and from where?" she asked, already on edge.

Smiling, he said, "The joint funds."

Nida's face dropped. "We're not touching those funds. I'm leaving in two months."

My father looked at me, seeking validation. "Tell her! You don't pass up on a good business opportunity that could double the money!"

I ignored him, a tactic I had learned was the best way to keep the peace. Annoyed, he turned back to Nida.

"There's a startup offering bonds with a 23 percent monthly return. No lock-in contract, and we can withdraw the original deposit at any time!"

"That makes no financial sense," Nida retorted.

"I'll take you to their office this afternoon. I've already spoken with their CEO. Think about it: we invest your tuition fees for one month, and by next month, we get 23% more!"

"That sounds dodgy!" she said.

"Because it is!" I chimed in.

Undeterred, my father continued, "They have a proper office in the city. I had to queue up with other investors just to meet the CEO. He's launching some sort of digital platform!"

Keep in mind, this was when tech startups were just gaining traction, mobile banking wasn't a thing in Bangladesh, and companies like Nvidia weren't worth trillions yet.

Nida hesitantly agreed, and later that day, they visited the company's office, meeting some of the 45 employees. It seemed legitimate on the surface, though their business model was clearly doomed from the start. Investors, however, saw it as an easy way to profit from someone else's bad decisions.

When Nida returned home, she looked flustered.

"What happened?" I asked.

"He's already invested all the money," she said, her voice shaky. "He only told me after introducing me to their employees."

"What?!" I was shocked.

"Yeah," she said, almost in tears. "I don't know how I'm going to sleep for the next four weeks. He said he'll withdraw the money then."

I'll spare you the suspense and jump straight to four weeks later. Nida had marked the date on her calendar. She memorised the process sheet the company provided for withdrawing the money—something that had to apparently be done in person. The day finally came, and we made our way to the office. It was on the fourth floor of a building in the city. As the lift doors opened, we were greeted by an empty office space under renovation, clearly being prepped for new tenants.

We didn't need anyone to tell us what had happened. Nida stood frozen, her face drained of all colour, her voice lost. My father, however, rushed downstairs to the building manager's office, desperate to find out if the company had moved to another floor. The manager's response was a devastating blow: "They only leased the place for one month."

He'd been scammed. Shocker!

In that moment, it became painfully clear how my father had gone bankrupt the first time—by making disastrous investments, trusting in schemes that were always too good to be true. It was the same story, repeating itself.

A recent news outlet had even run a piece about scams just like this: "Scammers have become increasingly sophisticated, luring individuals with enticing job offers and non-existent investment opportunities, often under the guise of working capital and partnership agreements, promising returns that are simply too good to be true." And now, we were part of that statistic.

My father was almost crushed with the weight of his guilt as he rushed back upstairs. Nida still hadn't moved, standing there as if time itself had stopped. She mumbled under her breath, "I'll never get out."

In a desperate attempt, my father promised, "I will sell whatever I can to get that money back into your account before you leave." He knew, as did we, that this meant financial ruin.

She said nothing.

True to his word, he swiftly sold everything in Naogaon that he had inherited through *Dadu*'s will, along with another portion of property in Pirojpur to the Al-Giri pharmaceutical company. The company now owned the majority of the land and leased out the remainder. I remember his son, Ibran, who was a thoroughly unpleasant person to be around which made selling our property to that family even less appealing to me.

My father kept two small houses from the deed, claiming they were meant to be rented out to families for a more diversified income, as he believed relying solely on Al-Giri was too risky. Ironically, however, he never managed to rent out the houses, or at least that's what he always claimed—hence his frequent absences, supposedly spent renovating the properties to make them seem more lucrative to tenants.

Nida got her money, but the cost was steep—perhaps steeper than any of us could truly grasp at the time. The rent my father received from the portion of the property still under his control *should* have been enough to sustain us comfortably. I emphasise *should*.

My sister flew to the UK. I wish I could say it was a heartbreaking moment at the airport, but the truth is, I couldn't bring myself to go see her off. Another choice I regretted only a day later. After he returned from the airport, my father sat me down at the dining table and said bluntly, "Leave school after year 10 and find work. I don't have any more money for you."

I knew the income from the pharmaceutical lease should have been more than enough to support us, so I challenged him, "I've done the math. The lease payments should comfortably cover at least two more years of schooling and living expenses."

But he cut me off. "That's *my* money, and this is *my* house. I decide what happens."

This might seem like a typical sentiment for some Western parents who wishes their children would leave and withholds their wealth until they die alone in a nursing home, complaining that no one visits. However, it's important to remember that my parents were Asian. In countries like Bangladesh, finishing school and attending university to acquire undergraduate-level skills isn't just a goal; it's a necessity for securing any sort of career stability both locally and overseas.

By this point, I had learned not to react to his provocations. I'd gone from being paralysed by fear to simply ignoring him, which probably frustrated him even more. He added, "I did what I had to for Nida because she chose to stay with me when her mother left. You did no such thing." The comment felt irrational.

"Because you killed mine before she had the chance," I lashed out still trying to keep the conversation rational. "But are you really going to cut me off midway through school?"

He leaned back in his chair, unmoved. "I don't have to do anything for you. I only kept you here because Nida insisted. Now, I don't need any of this. Be ready to leave."

His words hit me hard, but I stayed composed. I had learned by then that screaming or arguing would only escalate things. "If I leave," I asked carefully, "will you at least support me through to my A'Levels?"

His answer was final. "No."

There was no negotiating with him.

Two days passed. I waited for Nida to settle in and call me from the UK. As expected, she did.

"You finally got out!" I said, relieved.

"Yeah" she agreed.

Without wasting time, I laid it all out. "Can you please talk to him? Convince him to let me finish school before I leave. This kind of disruption will ruin my studies."

Nida paused before telling me, "I'll try but I'm not sure if he'll see reason. Be prepared for the worst."

"That's all I ask," I concluded.

Days went by, and while I spent hours after school with Sufi and the boys, I never brought up what was weighing on my mind. I chose not to tell them about Shahana, the young sisters, or how abusive my father was. As the Colonel always put it, such matters were best kept within the family and dealt with privately. It wasn't until much later that I had to explain to the boys about the arrangement we had with the Al-Giri family—simply because we knew the youngest Al-Giri personally.

The boys would laugh and joke around, but I just sat there, staring blankly, the future ringing in my head. Exam time had arrived—a month of exams—and although I tried to focus, one thought haunted me: *What will happen once I'm done with this?* While other students looked forward to the holidays, planning trips or time off, I feared what came next.

The large clock in front of the auditorium ticked slowly, just a few seconds shy of 2:00 pm, the end of my last exam. I stared at it, feeling a mix of gratitude and sorrow. Grateful because I had been more fortunate than many to even receive this education; sorrowful because it felt like I wouldn't be able to finish it. As soon as the bell rang, signalling the end, I didn't linger to talk to friends. I rushed home, but as I approached the building, I saw a moving truck parked outside. They were loading what looked like Nida's wardrobe—still decorated with the Barbie stickers from when she was little.

I went upstairs to find my father directing the movers. I felt a strange indifference—no anger, no relief—just numbness. He turned to me and said, "Nida was very insistent that I let you stay. Fine, I agreed to pay the rent if Nida covers your school tuition. Consider this my generosity for still choosing to provide for you."

What he proposed felt completely unreasonable. My tuition alone at that expensive school far surpassed Nida's earnings as a waitress in a UK bar after her bills were covered. I could see through it easily—it was just another one of his manipulative tactics to pressure Nida for daring to speak up on my behalf.

I took a moment to collect my thoughts, went to my room and dialled Nida. "Why did you say that? What about your studies?" I asked, curiosity mingled with irritation.

"I said what I had to," she replied coolly. "What matters is that you got what you needed. Make the most of it."

"But—"

"Nothing more," she insisted, her voice firm.

As I walked out of my room, I saw the last of Nida's furniture being carried out. "It's all going to Pirojpur," my father said. "I'll store it in the empty house on the property."

I didn't ask any further questions as I hadn't been to Pirojpur before. My father handed me some money as rent as he suggested that he will be moving to Pirojpur permanently and will only periodically drop by to give me my living expenses. Then, as he turned to go, he added almost as an afterthought, "Oh, and Chacha's gone. I dismissed him."

I stood there, in a half empty house, stunned. Not only was I—a fifteen-year-old—left to handle living alone, but he had also dismissed the one person who could have helped me. But what hit me hardest was that Chacha had been sent away without me getting to say goodbye. His village was far away, making it nearly impossible for me to see him again. I found out much later that not long after returning to his village, Chacha had passed away from pneumonia following a flood. That morning before school was the last time I saw him, though I didn't know it at the time. We often take our interactions with others for granted, never realising that those we speak to today may not be there for the next conversation.

I headed downstairs thinking about where to find contractors and movers, but my thoughts were interrupted by the sight of the car sitting in the driveway, coated in a fine layer of dust. It hadn't moved in months—not since Mizan left. I stood there, staring at it, thinking, *What am I supposed to do with this thing?*

I decided to ask my father. "What do I do with the car?" I asked over the phone. His reply was quick: "I gave it to your sister. Whatever she says, goes."

I sighed and dialled Nida via internet calling. "What do I do with the car?"

"Ask father," she said, her voice tinged with confusion.

"But *he* told me to ask *you*," I protested.

"Well, I'm telling you I have no idea."

I paused. "Should I just sell it?"

She laughed, "Who's going to buy a car from a fifteen-year-old without a license or a guardian? They'll think you stole it! But if you're serious, the registration papers are in my wardrobe."

Except the wardrobe was halfway to Pirojpur by now.

I called my father again, but he'd stopped picking up, probably annoyed by the whole situation. This was going nowhere fast.

Desperate, I called over my friend Shiro. He said he knew a thing or two about cars. Soon, we were both standing in front of the dusty vehicle, silently contemplating.

"So, no registration documents, huh?" he asked, glancing at me.

"Nope, just the keys," I said, shrugging.

""I know a few people who might be interested in buying it, but..." Shiro smirked. "Who's going to buy a car from a fifteen-year-old with no license or guardian? It's bad enough you live alone in that house—our 'respectable pious' elders would say anyone living alone is dishonourable."

He was being sarcastic, but unfortunately, he wasn't wrong. Many elders, lacking formal education, had managed to acquire land by doing menial jobs in the post-liberation boomer era, scraping by with minimal expenses and never stepping foot in a classroom. They bought properties for a pittance, often with the help of corrupt officials, and now controlled most of the land and assets. Their understanding of religion was rooted in old wives' tales and word-of-mouth—most had never read, or couldn't even read, their holy texts. So, naturally, their idea of honour was shallow, rooted more in societal appearances than an understanding of the complex circumstances behind them.

"Alright, alright," Shiro said, raising his hands in mock surrender. "But I think we need a third opinion."

Cue Sufi. Now there were three of us, all staring at the dusty car like it held the answer to some ancient riddle.

"I see only one solution," Sufi declared dramatically. "I know a guy who knows a guy who can chop it up and sell the parts."

We both shot him a look. Bringing Sufi into this had clearly been a mistake.

Sufi shot back, unamused, "I am not going to add grand theft auto to the list of alleged crimes that I should be convicted for. Let it sit here, Yaad. We'll think about it later when we're actually hard on cash"

Although my father had promised to provide my living expenses, he followed the same pattern he had when I was a child: supplying just enough for essentials but not enough to dine out, making cooking a necessity. I found myself spending time on the phone with Sufi's mother, who patiently guided me through recipes as I fumbled through my attempts. I ate whatever I could, and on weekends, she would send Sufi to my home with meal preparations.

My friends saw no issue with my situation though; they were thrilled to have a place where we could hang out unsupervised. We started playing football under the street lamps late at night that often followed with movie marathons at my place, with them bringing snacks. When I was home alone, I would immerse myself in books or focus on my studies. Reading always came naturally to me, and academics never felt like a struggle—something I was endlessly grateful for. We were making the most of our school holidays.

A month later, my father showed up unexpectedly. On his way up, the building manager mentioned that a group of delinquents had been hanging around our apartment, staying late into the night. It was clear he was referring to Sufi, Shiro, and Rajesh. In our culture, the concept of "mind your own business" or "I'll do what I want in the property I rented" often goes unheard. Instead, the perception of social character takes precedence. A religiously pious man, even if his actions were questionable, would never be challenged, while someone with a scar on their neck and a carefree attitude would quickly be labelled a delinquent.

My father's demeanour shifted instantly at the comment; he stormed upstairs and began yelling at me while I ate the dinner I had cooked.

His words cut deep, leaving me haunted and, despite my earlier indifference, feeling utterly suicidal. "Who gave you permission to bring them over? Did you ask me? You are a burden on me. I wish I had never cared for you. I give you a roof over your head, and this is how you repay me?" he shouted.

If you think he was being irrational, you would be right.

His familiar lip-squeaking began, a telltale sign that preceded his outbursts. I braced myself, preparing to defend against the verbal onslaught.

"WHAT DID YOU SAY TO ME?" he screamed out of the blue.

In reality, I hadn't said anything at all. "I didn't say anything. What are you talking about?"

He snarled, "I should kill you right here. If Nida hadn't made me promise, I would have probably done it!"

He then pulled out an envelope containing rent for the next four months, threw it at my feet, and turned to leave. He exited the building and didn't return for four months.

Despite my maturity, years of past trauma flooded my mind, and I found myself crying like I did when I was much younger and went without eating for the next two days. Unsure of what to do, I finally decided to call Nida. After I laid out the entire situation to her, she listened intently and then said, "Give me a moment. I'll call you right back."

An hour later, she called back, explaining that she had decided to send someone over, essentially acting as my caretaker for the next two years.

"We can't afford anyone," I protested.

"The person I'm sending won't ask for much," she replied. "Don't tell father, but your mom helped her finish her schooling. We've kept in touch by phone since your mom passed away."

Unable to hold back my curiosity, I asked, "Who?"

"Anna," she answered, naming *Dadu's* former caregiver. Anna had stayed on to help around the house after *Dadu* passed, and my mother had apparently transferred some money from my father's coffers to support Anna's schooling in secrecy. Grateful for the help, Anna eventually completed up to her year 12 of schooling. Nearly a decade later, when Nida reached out, Anna agreed to return. She did this so I could focus on my studies, all the while pursuing a nursing diploma of her own.

She became the single most important person to enter my life at that critical moment, offering support when I needed it the most. She helped me with groceries and cooking while studying at home during the day. Sufi enjoyed her company as she would go out of her way to cook treats for us like cookies and nuggets. She made her home on the floor of Nida's empty room and never complained about it. Knowing how much she loved to read, I subscribed her to a daily newspaper, a reading habit she maintained for years.

My father returned after four months. When Anna opened the door for him, he stared at her in disbelief and bluntly asked, "How is Ma's fever?"

Anna looked just as confused as I felt when he mentioned *Dadu* as I emerged from my room. "What?" she replied.

He fished around in his back pocket and stopped when he found something. After a moment of embarrassment, dismissed the question. "No, never mind. How are you, Anna? Thank you for helping Nida out," he said.

Realising there was no point in pressing the issue, I turned to him and asked, "How are you?"

In response, he pulled out two envelopes and threw them on the dining table—a noticeable upgrade from the last time he had tossed money at my feet.

"One envelope has the rent and some money for groceries for the next four months," he explained, "while the other contains the registration and insurance documents for the car"

"What should I do with them?" I asked, confused.

"Sell the car," he replied curtly, as if it were the most obvious solution. I wasn't surprised; it seemed like the most rational thing he'd said so far.

"Do you have any suggestions on where to sell it, to whom, or how much I should ask for?" I pressed, my sarcasm thinly veiled, unsure if he was mocking me or if he genuinely thought this was a reasonable request.

"Just sell it and give me the money. I need it," he said, his tone oddly drowsy.

"Wait, why do you need the money?" I inquired, but he merely said that someone was waiting for him downstairs and that he needed to leave.

Confused, I rushed to the balcony overlooking the street. I spotted a familiar face waiting on a rickshaw as my father exited the building and climbed aboard with him. It was Ranjan—the same person who had supplied him with maids. Ranjan was directing the rickshaw puller, while my father sat beside him, appearing unfocused.

Maybe I was too worn down to think much of it. I felt a strange sense of relief knowing I had received payment for the next four months, which meant he wouldn't return during that time. Once again, I chose not to follow up on this.

When the time came for what had now become regular payments, I was expecting my father to show up, as usual. Instead, he called. "I'll send you six months' payment via check today," he said in a cold, albeit confused voice, as if the mere act of sending money annoyed him. This was strange—he had never sent me a check before.

"Is something going on in Pirojpur?" I asked, recalling the unleased buildings he had mentioned in the past.

"Pirojpur?" he repeated after me, which only deepened my unease.

He didn't answer the question. Instead, he just said, "Call me when you get the check," and hung up. He didn't even follow up on whether I was able to sell the car yet.

The next morning, a courier arrived with an envelope. "*Odd*," I thought. It should have taken at least two or three days for this to arrive from Pirojpur. How did it get here so quickly? Unless it was sent from nearby. Even stranger, the envelope had no return address, which seemed reckless on his part.

I tried calling him after receiving the check, but he didn't pick up, even after I tried multiple times. I thought he'd return the call eventually, but days passed, and still, nothing. While it worried me, it wasn't entirely out of character. He resented me for reasons I still didn't fully understand, and I was in no rush to hear him lash out again.

Four months flew by in what felt like an instant. If you're wondering whether I had started dating at any point of time—being sixteen with an apartment of my own—the answer was no. This was a time when "room dates" were a common practice—teenage couples would rent rooms in rundown houses in shady neighbourhoods for an hour at exorbitant rates to satisfy their urges, as inviting their partners home was strictly taboo in the eyes of their parents. Anna would often leave for her placements after cooking meals to last me while she was away, so having someone over would have been easy. But I wasn't interested. I was too terrified of the inevitable question, "Tell me about yourself," and the uncomfortable follow-up questions that would come after. What I didn't realise at the time was that I had unknowingly learned and practiced another life lesson: Don't let bad experiences define your entire personality!

As I look back now, I saved myself from developing the habit of "trauma dumping" on anyone willing to listen. After navigating the dating world extensively, I have encountered so many dates who felt comfortable unloading their unresolved issues right from the start, expecting sympathy in return. Don't get me wrong—everyone has a story, and some are truly heartbreaking. My heart goes out to those who have suffered, but it becomes draining when, after empathising, I'd attempt to shift the conversation to something lighter, only to be met with frustration or offense.

What I noticed in my adult dating life was that some people made their trauma their entire identity. It wasn't just a part of their story—it was the only story! And while it's essential to talk about the hard things, it's equally important to strike a balance. If you need to offload deep emotional burdens, do it with a therapist, someone equipped to help you work through it: Don't drop it on someone who was just looking forward to pizza and a good time after a gruelling week! People naturally gravitate toward positive experiences, but it's the negative ones that tend to stick with them.

For me, I made it a point never to bring up my personal history or traumatic experiences on early dates. It was something I reserved for when I had built a solid connection, typically after several months. That's a principle I've stuck with—and I believe it's one worth living by.

Back to the story: four months later, I was preparing for my first round of A-level exams when the doorbell rang at 11:00 pm. Assuming it was Sufi or Shiro making a pitstop between places, I asked Anna to tell them to "go away." She smiled and walked to the door, but her smile quickly faded. She opened the door without saying a word. Puzzled, I peeked out from my room and saw my father.

That didn't make sense—there were still two months left on his payment. Why was he here?

He walked into my room, visibly groggy, slightly dragging his left leg as if it weighed him down. "I wish you were dead! When will you leave?" he spat, but this time, there was no lip-squeaking or trembling. His speech was slurred, and he struggled to keep his balance. Something was seriously wrong.

"Are you okay? Do you want me to take you to the hospital?" I asked.

"No! Just leave!" he shouted.

I stayed silent as he cursed at me for the next half hour, wishing terrible things upon me before finally dragging himself out. When he left, I did what had become routine: I went to the balcony and saw the same scene, this time under the street lamp—Ranjan, waiting on a rickshaw, this time helping my father climb aboard before sitting beside him and directing the rickshaw-puller where to go.

I turned away and focused on my studies. Again, I chose to let it go. Now wasn't the time for this. I needed to stay focused. I studied late into the night before switching off the light to catch some sleep.

The day of the exam arrived, and I stood outside the venue, ready to silence my phone and put it into my designated locker. Just as I was about to stow it, an unknown number flashed on the screen as my phone vibrated. There was no time to take the call, so I silenced it, figuring I could return the call after the exam.

Three hours later, I handed my paper to the exam invigilator and headed toward the locker to collect my belongings. As I picked up my phone, the screen lit up with 137 missed calls—all from the same number. A chill ran down my spine. This didn't seem normal. Before I could fully process what was happening, the phone rang again. It was the same number.

This time, I answered.

A woman's voice, shaky but urgent, said, "The Lieutenant has been admitted to Memorial Hospital. Come quickly!"

I got goosebumps. I knew the hospital, and deep down, I had sensed something was wrong the last time I saw him. If only I had known then what I knew now—I could have recognised the signs of a stroke. Maybe I could have told him to seek help sooner.

Just to confirm, I called my father's phone: It was switched off.

I rushed to the hospital, and when I reached the emergency waiting room at 6:30 pm, I scanned the room and noticed a pale, petite woman cradling a newborn baby, barely a month old, in her arms. Beside her, a five-year-old stood, staring blankly into space. There was something eerily familiar about the woman. She looked up at me, and in an instant, she seemed to recognise me.

It took me a moment to place her face. Then, like a flash, the memory hit me. I had seen her before—at *Dadu*'s bedside during her final days. She had been the caregiver, she was there with Anna, except for that one night when *Dadu* had become hysterical citing someone on the other side of her window wanted to kill her.

She knew I had recognised her. Her cold, fixed gaze remained locked on me, waiting for me to acknowledge her.

Almost unsure of my own voice, I mumbled, "Riba?"

Chapter 8. Return to sender

I stared at her in disbelief, the seconds stretching into what felt like an eternity. Finally, I broke the silence. "Is he inside?" I asked. She nodded, her expression cold and detached.

I walked to the medical officer's room, introduced myself as my father's son, and asked, "What happened to him?"

The medical officer pulled out my father's admission file, motioning for me to follow him to the lobby. He flipped through the pages before saying, "Your father suffered a stroke last night. In the following hours, it appears multiple organs began failing. We suspect he had a long history of undiagnosed high blood pressure, along with other untreated conditions."

"When was he brought in?" I asked.

He scanned the records, his expression growing more serious. "That's the troubling part. He was brought in this afternoon at 1:30 pm. We're uncertain if he collapsed unattended earlier in the morning, but he was brought here by that young woman in the corner and another man," he said, pointing toward Riba.

I glanced over at her, the questions swirling in my mind. "Who paid the deposit?" I asked, knowing the hospital wouldn't have started treatment without it.

The doctor nodded toward Riba again. "She did. She handed us a sealed envelope and instructed us to use the money inside. She was open about stating the money wasn't hers and she did not know how much was inside. I asked her where she got it, but she stayed silent. When I pressed whose money it was, she responded 'the Lieutenant's son.' We didn't argue. We had to proceed with treatment."

"Can I see the envelope?" I asked.

The medical officer pulled out the now-empty envelope from the file and handed it to me. I read the words scrawled on it: "For Yaad, the months of August to December."

He had set aside my payments, I realised.

The doctor continued, "That money was enough to start treatment, but we'll need more in the coming days. Since you're not of legal age, is there any family member who can sign the consent forms?"

I pointed to Riba. "Didn't she sign anything?"

The doctor shook his head. "She said she was not family."

I quickly remembered to ask, "What about his phone and other belongings?"

The doctor shook his head again, "He didn't have anything on his person when they brought him in"

"Alright. I'll call Colonel Mahmoud Oman, his brother. He'll handle the paperwork."

The medical officer seemed relieved and returned to his duties as I dialled the Colonel's number, explaining the situation. He assured me he'd be there in a few hours.

"*Perfect!*" I thought. That gave me just enough time to have a little chat with Riba. I needed answers.

As the ICU waiting room buzzed with activity, I approached Riba—now sitting in the corner, desperately trying to cradle the crying baby in her arms to sleep. Her sleep-deprived eyes stayed downcast, avoiding mine.

"Riba, I have questions," I said, breaking the silence.

She nodded, still not meeting my gaze.

"How are you here after all these years? You left that night!" I demanded.

Her voice was almost at the level of a whisper. "I wanted to leave, but in the end, I couldn't."

I couldn't help the accusation that slipped from my lips: "*Dadu's* room was ransacked, and someone tried to kill her. You set it up, didn't you?"

Riba's head snapped up, her eyes wide in defence. "No! I didn't mean for that to happen! I only found out much later."

I pressed on, not ready to let her off the hook. "The police said they found small footprints near my window, like someone was scouting the place for days. Was it you?"

"I envied your family," she confessed. "But at the same time, I felt sorry for you. The Lieutenant would beat his wife and daughter in front of us, and then at night..." She paused as I waited for her to continue.

"At night, he would have his way with us," she said flatly. "Each girl... on rotation. That's why so many left."

A chill ran through me. I asked, "Anna stayed with you till the end. Was she... involved?"

Riba shook her head. "No, Anna was never touched. But she found out."

"And what did Anna do?" I asked, trying to keep my voice steady.

"She told your mother and sister," Riba said. "Since then, I could see how they looked at me. I knew they were trapped, just like I was. But I was the only one left by then. They needed me, even if they hated me for it."

I needed to know more. "Why did you stay, Riba? Did he force you?"

Her answer was a slow shake of the head. "No. He never forced us. He offered the girls money—extra, for special favours. If they refused, he'd go to their families and make the same offer. It wasn't a threat, just money. And their families were too poor to refuse. Eventually, they convinced the girls to give in."

I stared at her, stunned. "What about you?"

She didn't flinch. "I didn't want to do it. But he offered a lot of money to my brother, and my brother said, 'It's only for a couple of nights. The money is good. It'll help rebuild the home we lost to the flood.' So I did it," she said, her voice cold, devoid of emotion. I expected her to break down, but she didn't.

She continued, "It was supposed to be five nights. The Lieutenant paid my brother in advance. He pushed me into doing it. The condition was, whenever the Lieutenant called, I had to go to his room and let him do whatever he wanted."

Her voice faltered, but she pressed on. "But it wasn't five nights for me. Soon enough, the Lieutenant offered my brother more money, and my brother agreed. Five nights turned into twenty-five over just a few months."

As uncomfortable as the conversation was getting, I had to keep going. "That still doesn't explain why you disappeared that night."

Riba's face hardened almost as if she knew exactly which night I was talking about. "I told my brother about..." She hesitated, her words catching in her throat. Whatever she was going to say, she swallowed it back, clamping her mouth shut. No matter how much I pushed, she refused to continue.

I realised I wasn't going to get the full story—not yet. So, I shifted my approach.

"Fine, so you left. But that doesn't explain why you're back now," I said, my voice laced with frustration.

Riba's eyes were hollow as she replied, "I could never really leave. When I ran back to my village, the Lieutenant found me. He offered my father enough money to build a poultry farm, something that would pull us out of poverty. All he wanted in return... was me."

Her words stuck to me, and I pressed her, "Go on."

"My brother saw it as an opportunity," she continued. "He told me, 'Riba Marya, I'll be by your side. We just need to stay long enough to get more help for the village. The more girls we bring, the less interested he'll be in you, and the more money we'll make overall.'"

I listened with a mix of shock and disbelief but was unable to look away as she revealed the full extent of her brother's complicity. "*He* kept half of what the Lieutenant paid for every girl that was sent in to serve as a maid. He would let the Lieutenant screen them first, and if he didn't like them, they wouldn't get the job."

"And how did you fit into all of this?" I asked, my voice barely concealing my anger.

"I was his favourite," she whispered, tears welling up in her eyes. "The Lieutenant wanted to keep me for years. Every time I wanted to leave, my family would force me to stay, saying we needed the money."

I remained silent, letting her speak.

Riba's tears spilled over, her voice breaking. "Everything changed when I found out I was pregnant. I wanted to get rid of the baby, but my brother—he saw the baby as leverage. He told me that with the baby, we could inherit everything the Lieutenant owned. My brother made sure I kept it a secret until the very end as he kept the Lieutenant distracted with other girls. By the time the Lieutenant found out, it was too late to do anything."

She gestured to the baby in her lap, her face twisted in pain. I asked, "What did my father do when he found out?"

"He was furious. With both of us," she replied. "But my brother got what he wanted. And me... I got stuck. I've been trapped in this nightmare for the last eight years, and possibly for the rest of my life."

I let her words sink in for a moment before asking, "So the other girls who came to work for us... you knew them?"

She nodded. "Yes, they were all from our district village. Even the two sisters Nida sent back. Ranjan wasn't happy about that. They were all from our village, except for Rabeya... she was from somewhere else, and had been there even before I was sent to him."

I processed her words carefully, then asked calmly, "So Ranjan Marya is your brother?"

Riba confirmed with a quiet, "Yes, he is."

I continued, piecing the puzzle together. "Why was he escorting my father around? I saw him with him several times."

Her voice sharpened with bitterness. "Ranjan wanted to know what properties the Lieutenant owned and what this baby"—she gestured to the child in her lap with evident disdain—"could inherit." The disgust on her face was unmistakable, and it was impossible not to pity the child. What kind of future awaits a child whose own mother doesn't want them? Riba's scene, though completely unique in its details, echoed the familiar story of young couples who believe a child can save their crumbling marriage, only to end up resenting the child even more than each other. Instead of a fresh start, they find themselves shackled to a new kind of baggage, one that makes leaving cleanly all but impossible.

But I digress. Riba's tone grew colder as she continued, "When he found out the Lieutenant had sold everything, he was furious. That's probably why he followed him—he was looking for assets the Lieutenant might have kept a secret."

A thought crept into my mind—had Ranjan been the one to pressure my father, driving him into the agitation and stress I had witnessed? I glanced at the boy sitting next to her, wondering how deeply this all went.

I glanced at the short, skinny boy sitting quietly beside her. "Who is this?" I asked, still trying to process everything.

Riba looked at him for a moment before answering, "He says his name is Beebo. The Lieutenant's son... from the other family. At some point, the Lieutenant brought him over to live with me. He never explained much beyond that. But Ranjan... Ranjan knows more."

Her words felt like one more addition to a series of revelations that had already left me numb. I barely registered what she was saying, and I asked bluntly, "Where is his mother?"

"You'll have to ask him," she replied, looking away.

I turned to the boy, trying to soften my voice. "Beebo, hi. I'm Yaad. Can you tell me where your mother is?"

Beebo met my gaze briefly, his eyes empty, and muttered, "She's gone."

That only raised more questions. "Where did you live before?" I pressed.

He glanced at me again and answered simply, "Pirojpur."

I realised I wouldn't get much more from him, and shifted my attention back to Riba. "The man who the doctor said came with you—was that Ranjan?"

She nodded.

"And where can I find him?" I asked, my tone growing sharper.

But Riba said nothing, only lowered her gaze. Just then, I noticed the Colonel walking into the room. His eyes briefly met mine, but he pretended not to acknowledge Riba or the children. Sensing the shift, Riba stood up, adjusting the baby in her arms. "I'll take my leave now. Thank you for answering my call."

I had so many more questions, but I knew there were more pressing matters at hand. I watched her walk away, and then turned to my uncle, who approached me with a look of quiet urgency. "Who's the duty officer handling Obik's case?" he asked.

After I introduced him to the fellow, the Colonel had a word with him and then returned, saying, "I'm going downstairs to make a deposit for two weeks. In the meantime, I'll make some calls to see if we can transfer him to the Military Hospital for free treatment as a veteran."

I nodded.

He continued, "But there's more. You should talk to Nida. A legal next of kin needs to come forward to draft his will, just in case he doesn't make it through the week."

"Is there a chance?" I asked.

The Colonel's face tightened. "From what I was told, even if he survives, his brain has suffered significant damage. It will likely deteriorate over time."

While waiting at the ICU waiting room, I had texted the boys to let them know what was happening and asked them to stay on standby in case I needed help. I deliberately avoided mentioning Riba by name, stating only that someone had brought my father to the hospital after his collapse, as I didn't want to make any assumptions without concrete proof.

Sufi called to tell me the group was already in the hospital lobby. When I made my way down to the hospital lobby, I found Sufi, Shiro, and Rajesh waiting, each offering their sympathies. I made a point to keep everything Riba had shared with me upstairs away from the boys; It felt deeply personal. As we talked, my phone buzzed with a call from an unknown number. I answered, but the reception was terrible with nothing but static crackling through the line from where I stood. As I walked away to get better reception, Sufi approached and, without a word, slipped a thick roll of money into my hand, closing it with his.

"Treatment must be very expensive, please take it" he said.

I stared at him, both touched and shocked at the stack he was handing me, before returning the money. "We're planning to transfer him to a military hospital where his treatment will be covered. But thank you for offering."

Sufi nodded in agreement.

Since he wasn't going to bring it up himself, I had no choice but to address the elephant in the room: "Sufi, where on earth did you get all this money?"

Sufi shrugged nonchalantly. "Don't worry about it. I know a guy who knows a guy who lent it to me."

I shot him a sceptical look. "Sufi, that's debt. You do know how debt works, right? You eventually have to pay it back. How were you planning to do that?"

He gave a sheepish grin. "I didn't think that far through."

I sighed, realising he was just like most people with a credit card—eager to spend money they didn't have on things they didn't need. But, despite the reckless spontaneity, I knew his heart was in the right place. I smiled, grateful for a few good friends who somehow managed to get you through life.

Sufi nodded. "I'll take my leave now. But remember, we're just one call away."

As he turned to leave, I called after him. "Make sure to pay back whoever you borrowed it from"

Moments later, the colonel came back and told me to go home and get some rest, warning we had long days ahead. I agreed.

After returning home, I went straight to the shower. From the other side of the door, Anna said, "Yaad, I heated up some food for you." She had no knowledge about my chat with Riba.

As I ate, I watched Anna read the newspaper, Riba's words circling in my mind. I wasn't sure if I should ask Anna about it yet—it felt premature. I needed to speak to Nida first, whenever she decided to call.

I got ready for bed, leaving my phone by my side. At 3:30 am, it rang. "I'm boarding my flight. I'll be there in two days," Nida said.

Half-asleep, I blurted, "What? Wait, don't do that!"

She replied, breathless, "Things are going to get really bad, and I can't leave you to handle this alone. Besides, he's my father too... for better or worse, he's all I have."

"You have a great life in the UK. Please, don't do this!" I said, guilt overwhelming me.

She cut me off. "If someone needs your help and you can offer it, you give it. We don't abandon people in need because we reap what we sow."

I knew where she'd learned that from, and it was clear her mind was made up.

"Please don't come back," I whispered.

"Yaad, you're the brightest person I know. You're not even eighteen yet. If you get caught in what's about to come, you'll never leave. But if I take over, you can focus on your future. As a girl, I can still get by marrying rich but our society expects educated men to be bread winners. No one is going to let you sit idle and feed you for nothing!"

I shot back, "Our society also has uneducated men married to maids who do nothing but beat their wives when they come back after 14 hour shifts around the city. That's not the point! Please don't ruin your life and come back."

She replied sarcastically, "that's not for you to decide. I am an *independent* woman perfectly capable of making my own bad decisions! And hey, if things don't work out, I can always put the blame on you!"

All I could say was, "I'm sorry."

"Don't be," she replied. "This is my burden to bear. After all, I chose him. Thankfully you never had to."

She hung up. Moments later, she texted me her flight details with the message: "Pick me up, will you?"

I replied, "Absolutely."

The next morning, I went straight back to the hospital. Riba was there, just as before, sitting with Beebo playing quietly beside her. She glanced at me, exhaustion etched across her face, clearly having not slept all night. She frantically tried to calm the baby in her arms, who was crying louder with every second.

"I don't have any money left," she said wearily, her voice strained over the baby's cries. "I asked Ranjan for help. He said he'd come over, but he won't offer any help for Beebo."

I looked at her, raising my voice to be heard over the wailing child, "How have you managed until now?"

The baby finally quieted down, allowing her words to come through more clearly. "The Lieutenant used to pay for everything. Ranjan convinced him not to give me any money directly, saying he'd take care of me when the Lieutenant was away."

"And?" I asked, my curiosity edging into frustration.

"Ranjan barely did the minimum—to feed the baby and keep him alive," she said, her voice hollow with resignation.

I hesitated for a moment, unsure where this conversation was leading. "What exactly are you asking me for?"

She looked up at me, her eyes pleading, "Please, take Beebo with you. If you do, it'll give me and the baby a fighting chance."

I paused, contemplating the gravity of what she was asking. But seeing the desperation in her eyes, I reluctantly agreed.

Riba turned to Beebo, her voice soft and broken, "Beebo, go with your brother. He will take care of you."

What I didn't expect was the sharpness in Beebo's response. "You're a useless b*tch, Riba. You can't even take care of me properly!"

I stared at him in shock, unable to process hearing such language from a young child. Riba sighed, almost as if she had been waiting for this moment. "He's just repeating what the Lieutenant said to me. Sometimes, Beebo even tries to hit me the way the Lieutenant did."

In that moment, the reality of how impressionable children truly are, hit me. No child is born a monster; they simply reflect what they witness and experience while growing up, especially how they're treated by their parents. If your child is healthy but being difficult, it's likely a reflection of how you've raised them.

"Why don't you discipline him?" I asked.

She looked at me, her expression pained. "I tried. But whenever I even raised my voice, the Lieutenant would get furious. Then he'd beat me instead. It was far worse."

I stood there, realising that this child needed far more discipline and care than I could probably give—especially as a sixteen-year-old. But still, I couldn't walk away from him. So I took Beebo's hand and agreed to take him in.

As Riba gathered her things and prepared to leave with the baby, I stopped her. "Riba, you said you never really left. Where did he keep you all this time?"

She hesitated, her face tightening. "I'm sorry, I can't tell you where. But I wasn't the only one kept there. I was just the permanent one."

"Why can't you tell me?" I pressed.

She lowered her voice as she replied, "Ranjan told me not to."

With that, she turned and left, just as she had the day before. And there I was, standing alone in the ICU waiting room, holding the hand of a six-year-old boy whose life had already been shaped by too much darkness.

I brought Beebo home, unsure of how to handle the responsibility that now rested on my shoulders. As I stepped inside, I told Anna to take care of him, knowing full well I wasn't equipped to parent. When she opened the door, Anna's surprise was evident, though her tired eyes hinted she wasn't as shocked as she appeared. She extended a hand to Beebo and gently led him inside, her expression calm.

Leaning closer to her, I whispered, "Discipline the child as you see fit."

Anna chuckled softly, shaking her head. "I don't think that'll be necessary," she said, her voice kind but firm as she playfully gave Beebo a stern look.

I held back any further advice and turned to Beebo, kneeling down to his level. "Anna will look after you," I said, trying to sound authoritative. "But you have to be respectful. Do exactly as she tells you."

Beebo gave a small nod, clearly more engrossed in the toy plane he was holding than in my words. That's when I noticed the plane—an old, worn pink fighter jet with a bent front wheel. My breath caught for a moment. It used to be mine!

I remembered that toy vividly. I used to run around with it when I was his age. In fact, I was clutching it the day I first saw my father hit my mother with a belt. That memory, long buried in the back of my mind, resurfaced with startling clarity as I watched Beebo's small fingers gripping the bent front wheel in the same way that I used to.

I went into my room and decided to call Anna in and share my concerns. I told her, "Riba told me everything."

Her voice was weary when she responded, "Yaad, there's always my side of the story, her side, and the truth somewhere in between."

"I know," I replied, unsure of what else to say.

She continued, "Your mother found out about Beebo and your father's other life a long time ago. When she confronted him, he beat her with a belt. Later she found out about Riba too. She asked him to make her leave, and he beat her again—this time, in front of Riba. I knew I had to leave; I just didn't know when or how. If your mother hadn't helped me with the money, I could have never gotten to where I am now. It's a shame she never managed to leave herself. And it's a regret I'll always carry that I could never go back to help her."

"I don't blame you. You did what you had to," I said. "But now, what do I do with the boy?"

"I spoke to Nida a few hours ago," she said. "Talk to her when she arrives, see what she thinks. If Riba won't take him in, maybe we can arrange for adoption—find a family that can actually love and care for him."

"I'm not sure he'd be welcomed anywhere," I said hesitantly. "He's been influenced by father's... habits."

"Whether he can grow out of it remains to be seen," she replied. "But you're struggling yourself. As painful as it is to admit, there's not much you can do for him, other than find him a home."

I sighed, knowing she was right. "I'll figure something out."

She added softly, "I hope you can get back to your studies. You need to leave before things get worse."

"That's what Nida said too," I replied, my voice trailing off.

Two days passed, and my father's condition remained unchanged. When Nida's flight landed, I went to the airport to pick her up. As she crossed through immigration, pushing a trolley with her luggage, I noticed she hadn't changed much in appearance—except for the worry etched into her face.

She unpacked, freshened up, and then sat down with Beebo for a private conversation in my room. I waited in the dining room as they spoke behind closed doors. I couldn't hear a thing.

When Nida emerged, she sat beside me and said, "I spoke to his mother. She's returned to her village. She barely has enough to feed herself, let alone raise Beebo. It looks like he'll stay with us. We should go buy at least a few beds until we figure it all out."

I frowned. "How are we going to afford that?"

Nida sighed. "The lease on the Pirojpur property should have provided enough income for a lavish lifestyle, but Father spent more than what he earned on his vices."

I stared at her. "How long have you known?"

Nida glanced over at Anna, who sat quietly on the sofa, then said, "For a long time. I never said anything. For a lot of reasons... but mainly because Father was all I had. He paid for everything and cared for me when everyone else left!"

Anna shifted uncomfortably as my sister spoke.

"Which account does the pharmaceutical make its payments to?" I asked.

"It used to be in our joint account but I'm not sure where the payment goes now," Nida admitted. "Let me call Hossein Al-Giri, the director. I have a list of father's important people and I'll be surprised if his name wasn't on it."

She dialled the number of the company director, Hossein Al-Giri—the man who had bought part of the Pirojpur property and was leasing the other. She raised the volume on her phone so she could hear, as she was almost deaf in one ear. This made the conversation on the other side clearly audible from where I was sitting.

After some brief, awkward pleasantries, Nida asked, "Uncle Hossein, which account do you make the payments to nowadays?"

The director responded with a chuckle. "What happened to the Lieutenant?"

Nida didn't hesitate. "He had a stroke. He's not doing well."

Al-Giri laughed again. "Poor Lieutenant. Don't mean to sound crude, but he deserved it! Last year, he cut power to my production line multiple times, claiming I was using too much electricity! I paid Mr Ranjan several times for that extra electricity. When I asked for an explanation, the Lieutenant gave me bizarre excuses!"

Without addressing Ranjan, Nida simply said, "He wasn't well. I'm sorry for what happened. We'll be taking over from here."

The director's tone turned cold. "He cost me hundreds of thousands with that stunt. I'm not paying a cent unless—" And then he hung up.

Nida looked at me, frustrated. "He's trying to take advantage of Father being out of the picture. He thinks we can't do anything."

I nodded. "He mentioned Ranjan."

Anna chimed in from across the room, her voice almost a rant, "Riba's brother? He'd sell his own mother for a bottle of top-shelf vodka. All he cares about is money and wanting to live the high life!"

Nida sighed. "I think Ranjan pocketed the payments instead of passing them along. That's probably why the electricity was cut."

Anna shook her head. "Sounds like something he would do."

"There's no point getting into this just yet," Nida said, visibly tired. "I've got some money Let's get a few beds at least for Anna, Beebo, and myself."

"And until then?" I asked to which she responded, "Beebo and I will sleep on the bed and you'll make do on the floor, obviously!"

"*obviously!*"

In a few days, Nida received a call from a lawyer. Al-Giri had sued us, claiming father had sold him all of the Pirojpur property, except for the two small buildings in the corner. Nida was furious, certain it was a lie. He was clearly trying to execute a hostile takeover now that father was incapacitated; That was what happened to many of the farmers when Uttara was developing.

"We need the legal documents to contest this," Nida said, pacing. "But they're locked in the safe hidden inside my wardrobe." I knew the one, the wardrobe with the Barbie stickers that the movers hauled away to Pirojpur after she left!

I stared at her. "The documents were with you this whole time?"

She nodded. "I was always dragged into this deeper than I ever wanted to be. Father told me he sent everything I owned to Pirojpur. It's probably in one of the two residential buildings that he was trying to renovate. And I'm willing to bet that's where Beebo lived too."

She called out to Beebo in the same sharp, commanding voice our father used. It struck me as odd, but I figured it was her way of asserting authority now. Beebo rushed over, and Nida asked, "We're thinking of going to Pirojpur to see your home. Do you think you could be our tour guide?"

His face lit up with pride at the responsibility, and he eagerly replied, "Yes!"

Without wasting any time, we called Rajesh to drive us around for the day. He was the only person I knew who could drive and was always just a call away. While waiting for him to arrive, I dusted off the old Toyota sitting idle in the garage. Sufi was right not to have his guy chop it into pieces. I tried calling the guy but he just wouldn't pick up.

Once Rajesh showed up, we were ready to set off for the Pirojpur property, with Beebo as our guide. Rajesh roped Shiro into coming along, likely for company, but I suspect they wanted to serve as muscle in case things went south while we explored the shady Pirojpur property. Though Nida had been there once as a child, I had never seen the place, and neither of us knew what to expect now.

As the car sped down the highway, I figured it was as good a time as any to ask.

I glanced at Nida and hesitated before blurting out, "Hey, did you ever make father promise not to kill me?"

She looked at me, half-smiling, thinking I was joking. "Very funny. I know he's grumpy, but he'd never want you dead!"

"No, but he did," I pressed. "He told me once—said you made him promise not to."

Her smile faded, replaced by concern. "We never had that conversation," she said, her voice soft. "Maybe you misheard him."

"Right," I replied sarcastically. "Because there are so many things that sound like '*I should've killed you if I hadn't promised Nida I wouldn't.*'"

I watched Shiro smirk from the front passenger seat, but neither he nor Rajesh said a word or asked any questions during the entire journey. The boys didn't ask for any personal details, and Nida decided it was best not to talk about Riba or Ranjan in front of the boys, or who Beebo really was, in an effort to preserve whatever shred of dignity our father still had left. I honestly saw no sense in that, but I complied.

We both fell silent after that, realising we weren't going to get any answers. Staring out of our respective windows, we let the moment of silence hang, as Beebo sat between us, oblivious, happily playing with my...*his* pink fighter jet.

Nida traced the address to the Pirojpur property from a list of contacts among my father's important documents. Google Maps hadn't fully mapped Bangladesh back then, so we had to stop several times to ask for directions. Finally, we arrived at the bustling, narrow streets of a rural town centre in Pirojpur. Beebo peered out the car window and pointed eagerly at a tall-walled, gated property. "We're home!"

We parked by the gate and got out while Shiro and Rajesh waited in the car. The door to the property was locked. Nida knelt beside Beebo, asking, "How do you usually get in when your father isn't here?"

"The uncle from the laundromat next door lives here. He rents from father and lets me in when I get locked out," he replied, then innocently ran ahead to ask for help. We followed him to the laundromat, where the owner, Siddiq, immediately recognised him.

"Beebo! I haven't seen you or your father in almost a year! How are you?"

I leaned toward my sister and whispered, "A year?" She gave me a quiet gesture to stay silent.

Beebo introduced us. "Uncle Siddiq, these are my brother and sister. Can you let us in? I want to show them our home."

Siddiq hesitated, clearly uncomfortable, but agreed. As we walked toward the gate, he said, "The Left-ten-ant hasn't been here in almost a year, and I haven't seen the boy's mother either. Why are you here now?"

"My father sent some things here, and we're here to take them back," Nida replied casually.

As Siddiq unlocked the gate, he added, "Tell your father the place needs repairs. Everything is falling apart."

Inside, Beebo ran ahead, excited to show us where he used to play. But what greeted us was a courtyard overrun with weeds, littered with dead leaves and cracked concrete. The building itself looked neglected, with broken locks and a torn net over the door. Yet Beebo's enthusiasm was undiminished, running from place to place, pointing out his favourite spots.

"Like I said," the laundromat owner commented, "no one's been here in a year. Feel free to look around, though."

We stepped into the house, which was dark and thick with dust. Spiderwebs clung to the ceiling, and ants swarmed over rotting fruits on the table. Cockroaches scurried in and out of cracks in the walls. Beebo, oblivious to it all, dashed from room to room, describing what he used to do in each one.

Nida flipped a switch, half-expecting no electricity since the pharmaceutical director had told her the power had been cut. But the lights flickered on. Surprised, she asked the laundromat owner, "Who's paying the bills for this place?"

"I cover the compound's utilities. Ranjan's responsible for the rest," he said.

My sister continued searching the rooms, looking for familiar furniture. Beebo proudly led us to a playroom where I saw old toys from my childhood, strewn across the floor. Even my old bed was there in a corner, though now broken and covered in dust. But none of Nida's belongings were anywhere to be found.

"Do you know where the furniture that was moved here a year ago is?" she asked Siddiq.

He looked puzzled. "Miss Nida, no new furniture's come here in the last five years."

"Are you sure?" she pressed.

"Yes, Miss. No one gets in without me letting them in."

Nida, now visibly uneasy, stepped outside to get some air, surveying the crumbling courtyard and the barbed wire that separated the compound from the pharmaceutical factory behind it. She seemed to have an epiphany, spinning back toward the laundromat owner.

"Where do you send your rent now?" she asked.

"Oh, didn't the Left-ten-ant tell you? A year ago, Ranjan came by and told me to send the rent to a new address. I confirmed it with your father over the phone the first two times, and he said he got it. I haven't asked since, and he hasn't contacted me about it."

Nida stood in silence for what felt like an eternity, before finally asking, "Can I see that address?"

Siddiq nodded and led us to his office, pulling a diary from a drawer. He flipped through the pages and pointed to an address in Uttara. But it wasn't one we recognised from any of our homes.

"It's worth checking out," I suggested. She nodded in agreement.

Before we left, Nida gave Siddiq her bank details. "Send the rent here from now on," she instructed. "And call the police if Ranjan shows up again."

He glanced at Beebo, who was now playing quietly with a toy from the house. "Okay," he said with a resigned sigh.

We left Pirojpur and followed the address we'd been given to an unfamiliar part of Uttara. This side of the city wasn't as developed as the rest—likely a low-rent area meant to support the working class. As we entered the neighbourhood, Shiro remarked, "This is a really bad neighbourhood. Sufi's weed dealer lives here!"

Still, we pressed on, arriving at a dingy building tucked in a narrow alley. "The car can't go in" Rajesh said.

"That's fine. We'll walk from here. Come on, boys," Nida called to Beebo and me.

We stepped out and made our way down the cramped alley on foot, eventually reaching the building. Climbing the stairs to the third floor, we found the only apartment. But before Nida could knock, Beebo suddenly exclaimed, "Why are we at that b*tch's house?"

Nida looked shocked and confused at Beebo's sudden use of profanity, but I understood. "He means Riba. This is probably where they've been staying."

I felt uneasy. Anything could happen once we were inside. As paranoid as it might sound, I called Shiro and instructed him to call me in fifteen minutes. If I didn't answer, he was to call the police.

After hanging up, Nida knocked on the door. There was no doorbell, but the door creaked open with just one knock. "It's unlocked," she said, pushing it further.

"Aren't we trespassing?" I asked, but she hushed me.

Beebo, unaware of the weight of it all, ran ahead and pointed to a small room in the corner. "This is where Riba stayed!" he exclaimed. The room was almost barren—just a torn mattress on the floor, a plastic table with a few pieces of cutlery, a single chair, and an old 14-inch television on a rickety stand. Despite the bare essentials, everything was neatly arranged, the bed carefully made, and the room spotless, as if someone had been living there until very recently.

Beebo led us to the next room. "This is where father used to keep our other guests," he said.

We knew what he meant. Inside, three torn mattresses lay scattered on the floor. The curtains were in tatters, and the small window looked out onto the wall of the neighbouring building. The room felt stifling, claustrophobic, with nothing else in sight but decay.

Beebo led us to the room across the hall, his small hand resting on the door. "This is where Father stayed," he said quietly. I noticed the tower bolt beneath the doorknob, with a padlock hanging from it. It was the same old, rusted padlock with the red accent stripe that, as a child, I saw him use to lock his room when he would be away.

"He used to have a bed and a metal trunk in here." Said Beebo.

"*The same bed and trunk I remembered from when we all lived together,*" I thought.

Beebo continued, "That was until he forgot how to use the bed and started sleeping under it. Then Ranjan came and took it away. He said Father slept better on the floor." With that, he pushed the door open.

The room was almost empty. The trunk stood open, a few shirts and pants spilling out, but it looked desolate. The walls bore deep scratches, and there were patches of dried dirt and what appeared to be red stains. The stench hit us—a rank odour like the back alleys of a nightclub or a cheap massage parlour. It reeked of neglect and desperation.

We stepped inside, spotting a bedpan abandoned next to the trunk. I knelt to peer inside the trunk—just a few of our father's cheaper clothes remained, wrinkled and unwashed.

I turned to Beebo. "Are these all the clothes Father had?"

Beebo scratched his head, confused. "No, he had more. But Ranjan took them away. He said Father didn't need them anymore."

This was my father's real base of operations. All those times he claimed to be in Pirojpur, how many of those were lies? How many times had he been here instead, just a few kilometres from us, hiding in plain sight for months? He had turned this apartment into his own sordid playground, a den for his concubines. And in the end, my father had been reduced to a prisoner in the harem he had built for himself.

Was he losing his mind in those final days? It would explain his irrational behaviour, his growing paranoia, the way he had unravelled.

Nida remained silent, arms crossed tightly as if hugging herself, as we walked through the apartment, taking in each detail with stunned disbelief. Beebo, unaware of the tension in the air, led us innocently to the last room in the dark corridor. "This is my room!" he said proudly.

Inside, we found Nida's old bed, a small wooden study table, and a child-sized chair. Against the wall stood a wardrobe, decorated with familiar Barbie stickers. Nida's wardrobe.

Without hesitation, she ran to it and flung the panel door open. The flimsy wood splintered and broke off in her hand. Gasping, she looked down and found the hidden wooden compartment at the base smashed open. The chest that had once been inside was gone.

They had fled, taking everything with them.

Beebo, blissfully unaware of the gravity of what was happening, continued with his innocent tour. He pulled the little chair up to his small table and sat down with a satisfied grunt. "Father bought me this table when he first brought me here," he said proudly. "I do all my school homework on it. It's great!"

As Nida knelt beside the broken wardrobe, lost in her own world of shock, I heard a scratching noise. I turned to see Beebo sitting at his little table, trying to peel away something stuck on the corner with all his might. Curious, I moved closer and crouched down beside him.

He was struggling with a small sticker, peeling it off piece by piece. As I looked closer, I could make out part of the faded label that still clung to the wood: "okbu."

I was petrified. I knew that tasteless sticker.

Shaken, I stood up and rushed back to the room where Beebo had said father kept his "guests." I knew what I was looking for and where to look. I knelt beside the mattresses, lifting the worn fabric, and there it was—the same sticker on each one. The same sticker I had on my own bed. On every piece of furniture, I owned: "Mokbul Furnitures"

Mokbul had known all along! The unease I'd sensed in him now made sense—he had probably seen this very apartment and was shaken up by all its secrets. He had known the truth, and he had been too afraid to speak.

Shiro called, just as I had instructed, but his question was absurd: "Are you okay, or did Sufi's weed dealer get to you?" Rajesh's voice came through the speaker right after, "Did you find Sufi in there?"

I brushed off their jokes and reassured them that we were fine, telling Shiro to expect us back in thirty minutes.

Unsure of our next steps, Nida called the Colonel to explain the situation. He listened patiently before responding, "I don't want to get involved. I'll ensure he's taken care of at the hospital, but his personal affairs should be handled by family."

Feeling lost, we ventured downstairs and knocked on the door of a neighbouring apartment. A weary woman answered, revealing she was a nurse who worked long hours and rarely saw anyone come or go.

"Do you know who owns the third floor?" my sister inquired.

"The entire building belongs to one person. I can give you their contact information if that would help," she offered. We accepted her offer and settled into the car as Nida made the call and we stared on at the road in front of us. A few moments later, an elderly gentleman stepped off a rickshaw. He wore a long white thobe or "jubba", and his thick, religious beard framed a face of quiet authority. He was the building's owner.

As we walked to the apartment, we asked him what he knew about the tenants. "I only know that a retired army man and his daughter rented the apartment. It was under the Oman's name, but I heard his daughter often had friends over," he replied.

Entering the home, he looked around in shock and asked, "What's going on here?"

Nida crafted a half-truth, "The Lieutenant had a stroke and is fighting for his life. We came to find his daughter to deliver the news, but discovered the place in this state. Can you help us locate her?"

The landlord shook his head, "I don't have cameras on the premises. Have you contacted the police?"

Realising we had no leads on Riba or Ranjan, we shook our heads. All we had was a phone number that was no longer in service. Back then, in Bangladesh, phone numbers didn't need to be registered to an individual, and they could be bought at a grocery store just as easily as they could be discarded. We then asked him to cancel the tenant agreement and keep the bond money for damages. Seeing our distress, he generously offered to return the bond money to my father's bank account without hesitation, an account to which my sister had joint custody and was now in control of. What a good man!

With new clarity, we headed to the police station, but it turned into a dead end; we lacked the evidence or coherent descriptions to file a report. Our next stop was the government land and development services to report the stolen documents.

At the clerk's desk, we were presented with a hefty folder containing records for the Pirojpur estate. As he flipped through the pages, he looked up, "This property has a massive unpaid loan that has ballooned to three times its original value. Were you aware that Mr Oman stopped paying the mortgage a few years back?"

Nida whispered, "No, sir, I didn't."

It hit me then: my father might have been forgetting to make payments, or perhaps he delegated it to Ranjan who had simply misunderstood what the deposits were for.

The clerk continued, "Currently, the land is being contested, and a lot of powerful people are waiting for the property to be auctioned off when the mortgage isn't paid by the deadline."

He removed his glasses and rubbed his tired eyes, adding, "Miss, the person who stole those documents clearly has no idea what kind of administrative mess this property is in. If they want it, they'll need to pay the debts and possibly go to court."

A mix of frustration and dark humour washed over us. "When Ranjan discovers that the documents he stole will bring him more trouble than he anticipated, I wonder how he'll react," I mused.

Later, we met with our lawyer to inform him that we would no longer contest the lawsuit against Al-Giri's pharmaceutical, effectively allowing the opposition to win uncontested once the loan repayment deadline passed in one-and-a-half years. While the court ruled in favour of the pharmaceutical, they mandated that Al-Giri pay rent for the duration until deadline, adjusted for the costs incurred during the electrical disruptions, until the repayment period expired. Our partial victory was largely due to the timing of the ruling—Al-Giri's reputation had recently been tarnished by a scandal that dragged them through the mud. Karma, it seemed, was on our side!

Additionally, we began receiving rent from Siddiq, the laundromat owner in Pirojpur.

We had bought ourselves just enough time to figure things out. Life carried on. Nida resumed caring for our father during the day at the military hospital, while spending her evenings applying for jobs. Beebo stayed with us, attending a local public school, but he often got into trouble, picking fights with other children. Each time, Nida, the only legal adult in the house, was called to the principal's office. Beebo would justify his behaviour by saying he was merely imitating what he had seen our father do at home. We didn't know how to help him. Mental health therapy in Bangladesh, especially for children, was rare, mostly privatised, and far beyond our financial reach.

Months passed, and my father's condition improved enough for him to move from intensive care to regular supervision and eventually to the officers' ward. Finally, the doctors told us he could go home, though he'd need to stay on heavy medication. They warned that his brain had suffered irreversible damage and would continue to deteriorate.

Nida brought him home and set him up in the same room as Beebo, and Beebo was thrilled to have him back. I couldn't understand how he was so at ease with my father's presence. "Surely he has Stockholm syndrome," I'd mutter to myself. But that's the thing about children—they love their parents, for better or worse. Tough luck for the ones stuck with parents who are incompetent, clueless, and utterly unfit to raise a goldfish, let alone a child. Yet, they still decide to reproduce and drag more lives into their chaotic wake. Honestly, not everyone is cut out to be a parent. And I say that fully aware I wouldn't exist if Lieutenant Oman had just gotten a vasectomy!

Life under Nida's supervision wasn't all that bad. Yes, she was controlling and liked to micromanage, but it never felt suffocating. She had just landed her first job after returning to Bangladesh and reconnected with Kaushal, the guy who fed me chicken all those years ago! They started meeting after work, and he'd drop her home in the evenings. Meanwhile, Beebo and I went to school during the day. After school, I'd play football in the evenings, while our father lay in bed most of the time. He wasn't entirely bedridden, but his deteriorating health meant we all had to take shifts to look after him. My sister would give him his morning dose before heading to work, I'd take over in the afternoons after school, and she'd clean him up and handle his final medications before calling it a night. Anna managed the household, helping with our father just as she had with *Dadu*, and took care of Beebo when he returned from school. The problem was, this quickly turned into a full-time responsibility, leaving her little to no time to focus on her own studies, which had been the original plan. The weight of caring for all of us made it increasingly difficult for her to balance her own ambitions of becoming a certified nurse.

Anna had started deferring her courses because she hadn't had time to prepare for the prerequisites. Seeing how caregiving and housework had taken over her life, I asked her to resign. At first, she hesitated, unwilling to abandon us. But I was forceful, letting my frustration turn into anger. My words hurt her, and though I hated myself for it, I didn't see another way. It was a tough, ugly decision—one that made me seem villainous even to myself. That was the last meaningful conversation we ever had. She stood outside the gate for what felt like an eternity, her luggage by her sides, waiting for me to change my mind and invite her back in. From my balcony, I could see her standing there, and my heart ached with every passing moment. Yet, I turned away, standing firmly behind the choice I made that day. Perhaps she still despises me for the harsh words I spoke before asking her to leave, words that I regret but will not take back; They had to be said.

By then, I had already begun training for the military, going through intense physical drills every day hoping to get enlisted. You might wonder—*hasn't he had enough*? Despite my complicated relationship with my father, I grew up in a household governed by military discipline and rationing. As much as I disliked him, he had subconsciously become my role model during my most impressionable years. It's like how children born into households of addicts are more likely to develop the same destructive habits as adults—It's a gift that just keeps on giving, whether you want it or not! Thankfully I was not selected for the military!

Sufi introduced me to his mother in person, and it was an odd but heartwarming experience—we bonded almost instantly. She reminded me so much of my own mother: a selfless, caring woman who always put others before herself. She would cook for me, and I loved spending Fridays with Sufi's family. For my Western readers, Fridays and Saturdays were our official weekend days, unlike the Saturday-Sunday weekends common in the West.

Sufi and I would play chess while his mother shared stories about their family. One day, she told me about Sufi's twin sister, Sammy, who had gone to sleep one night and never woken up. It was a tragedy that clearly haunted Sufi, as he had never mentioned it to me. My heart ached for them as Sufi's mother recounted Sammy's dream of becoming a doctor and earning a doctorate. She then looked at me and said she saw the same intellect in me that she had seen in Sammy.

Validation only truly matters when it comes from those who genuinely care about you, and her words meant everything to me at that moment. Talking to her felt like talking to my own mother—but in a different form.

Sufi's mother's advice found a permanent place in my mind, and I finally saw some sense. I took the national medical entrance exam—and to my surprise, I got accepted to a teaching hospital in the city of Sylhet! Unfortunately, Sufi and I couldn't pursue medicine together like he had always wanted, as he ended up having to repeat year 12 because of a persistent health issue that the doctors were struggling to diagnose. We gradually lost touch. The 250-kilometer distance between us, combined with my own growing commitments, made it impossible for me to help him with his studies anymore. Still, I kept convincing myself that one day I would become a doctor and help diagnose and treat Sufi's condition.

I developed a habit of falling asleep to YouTube videos—mostly to improve my English vocabulary and pronunciation. This was back in the days before tasteless prank videos and TikTok dance influencers flooded the platform, so the content was largely educational. It was my belated attempt to address the critiques I had received in school, where teachers often pointed out that my writing lacked polish. They weren't wrong; my English proficiency test scores at the time confirmed as much.

And here I am, a surgeon with two degrees under my belt and pursuing a PhD in Australia. I guess the joke's on English! Of course, most English proficiency tests have the convenient feature of expiring after two years, implying that once they do, we magically lose the ability to read or write the language! Naturally, this means we have to take yet another exam to reassure our Western counterparts that we still know how to spell our own names.

Thanks to Nida's support, I completed school and eventually moved out in a year and earned several academic accolades. The stereotype often perpetuated in older Asian cultures—that children from broken families are doomed to fail—no longer holds water in today's world. In fact, I believe such children mature faster, often gravitating toward one of two extremes: some spiral into bad choices and substance abuse, while others rise to remarkable success. However, even those in the latter group often carry lasting psychological scars, ranging from mild insecurities to more profound conditions like narcissism, sociopathy, or "daddy issues."

Fortunately, I think landed on the positive side of that spectrum, thanks to the incredible women in my life who stepped in to guide and support me. Not everyone is as fortunate, and I remain deeply grateful for their influence. Through persistence and determination, I earned a scholarship to study in Australia—an opportunity that felt like a turning point in my life. Interestingly, it was Sufi who first planted the idea of pursuing higher education, even though he never could pursue one himself. Life has an odd way of working out, doesn't it?

Nida would call me once every week with updates about her life. Nida and Kaushal were planning to get married, and I was genuinely happy for her. "That's great!" I said once. "But what about father and Beebo? What happens to them?"

She reassured me, "Kaushal's agreed to help. We'll all move in together—him, his aging mother, our father, and Beebo. We'll have this big, blended family from all over the place!"

"And he's okay with that?" I asked, still in disbelief.

She laughed. "Yes! I told him that I didn't want gold or jewellery as wedding gifts. All I asked of him as prenup was to help me hold on to whatever family I have left... though I phrased it less desperately, of course."

They got engaged and married quickly, and I was there for it all—helping with the logistics, attending the ceremonies.

One day, I received a call from a number that wasn't saved in my phone. This was before services like Truecaller were common, so answering the phone always carried an element of surprise. The only thing I can assure my Western readers is that it wasn't someone pretending to be from Vodafone Australia, claiming I'd spent $400 on Amazon and urging me to install a screen-sharing app so they could "log in" to my Commonwealth Bank account, fix the issue, refund the money through PayPal, and throw in a discount on my next electricity bill! Bangladesh simply wasn't wealthy enough to attract the attention of international scammers.

I picked up the call, and a familiar female voice broke through the static. "Yaad?"

I recognised her instantly, but how she had gotten my number was a mystery. I initiated the conversation as blandly as possible, considering the mess they had left us in. "Riba, how did you get my number?"

"It was saved on the Lieutenant's phone," she replied.

Of course. The doctors had told us that my father hadn't had any personal belongings when he was brought into the ICU. Maybe she had kept the phone for herself.

"I called Nida, but she wouldn't listen," Riba continued, "Now she's stopped picking up my calls. Please, I beg you, ask her to call me back."

"What won't she listen to? I need more context," I pressed on.

A moment of hesitation lingered in her voice before she spoke out. "The baby and I are out of money. Ranjan stopped supporting us. Please tell Nida to help—not for me, ask her to do it for her little brother."

I seized the moment to press further. "So, I suppose the property documents weren't helpful?"

Riba's slip was almost imperceptible. "No, they—" Then she quickly recomposed herself. "I did what I was asked to do, I'm sorry. I had no choice."

"That's not an answer," I shot back, frustration boiling in me.

"Please," she pleaded, desperation creeping into her voice. "Ranjan says he's got no more money to give me."

I pressed, unable to resist. "Didn't Ranjan share any of the gold he stole from *Dadu* with you?"

She abruptly hung up before I could press further. When I tried calling back, the phone was switched off. Was she afraid she'd reveal too much, or was someone else listening and decided to end the call for her?

Riba never called back—neither me nor Nida.

Chapter 9. All I have

I arrived in Sylhet to start my medical school classes. Some of my classmates jokingly referred to themselves as "20 percent doctors" after completing their first year, adding another 20 percent with each subsequent year passed. In hindsight, I realise that completing medical school alone doesn't make you a doctor. It's your ability to adapt to ever-changing situations while delivering effective treatment that truly defines you as one.

The entrance exam for medicine and surgery had limited seats, reserved for the best of the best. Yet, half of those who got in dropped out within the first three years. That taught me an important lesson: being a doctor is less about merit and more about persistence and resilience. The clinic hours were long, and the days never seemed long enough to prepare for the exams that loomed constantly over us. Yes, we had assessments almost every day, either during classes or after student clinics.

The workload became so overwhelming that I gradually lost touch with Sufi, Shiro, and Rajesh, barely managing to speak to Nida once every weekend after clinics. After all, who better to staff hospitals on weekends than interns and student doctors?

In my final year, I expressed interest to pursue surgery, and was placed in a rural village. While doctors have the option to work in rural areas, most avoid it due to the lack of proper facilities and resources. Does that make us bad people for wanting a better life after years of relentless turmoil? The locals, however, often held a different perspective, blaming doctors—or the lack of them—for all their misfortunes.

One of my seniors, a fresh graduate, experienced this firsthand when he was attacked by villagers for not responding quickly enough to a child who had been hit by a bus while playing on the highway. The child's injuries were severe, and realistically, there wasn't much he could have done, but being a fresh graduate, he fumbled under the pressure. It was his first real case of handling road trauma without supervision.

And why was he unsupervised? My senior's supervisor was a government-appointed doctor who rarely showed up. She would visit the village once every two or three weeks, just to sign off on paperwork for the rest of the month, while they focused their efforts on private practices in the big cities. Being a gazetted officer in Bangladesh meant their jobs were secure, and accountability was minimal.

Adding to the challenges, our supervisor was the only gynaecologist in the area. Her absence left my colleague and me responsible for women's sexual health—a task neither of us minded, but one that the villagers found culturally unacceptable. For them, discussing their intimate lives with male doctors was taboo, yet ironically, they were perfectly comfortable confiding in female doctors, regardless of the actual expertise. It was one of the many ironies we faced in those rural postings, where culture often collided with care.

In the Western world, sex education is provided to ensure teenagers make informed decisions. In contrast, sex education is almost non-existent in the Eastern world, where rural teachers sometimes go as far as stapling pages mentioning human genitalia as the first exercise when classes start. Naturally, this sparks more curiosity, as forbidden fruits are always the sweetest.

Once, a young girl claimed she was raped by a boy behind her family barn. She came straight to us, and we involved the police. To prove the boy's guilt, we needed a sample of his semen that he had ejaculated inside her to be sent to a lab for confirmation. However, the police intervened, stating that it was culturally inappropriate and that they would rather wait for our supervisor to arrive in two weeks, even allowing the semen to fester in the woman during this time. Any swab tests conducted after two weeks would no longer be helpful, and there was nothing we could do about it. The woman ended up pregnant, and the girl's family, in their infinite wisdom, decided to marry her off to her assailant to avoid bringing shame upon themselves. What could possibly go wrong in this so-called "perfect" happy ending?

When I wasn't assisting surgeries, I was stationed in the outpatient clinics. One day, a couple came in and told the reception that the man had come down with an unexplained cold. When I asked about their concerns, the man admitted that they had fabricated the symptoms because they wanted to discuss something more sensitive.

The man, nearly in his 40s, had recently married a girl who was not even of consenting age. In rural villages, this was sadly common, as arranged marriages differed drastically from those in the cities. In these communities, girls had almost no say in whom they were married off to. Younger men were rarely considered as potential grooms because they needed years to become financially stable enough to support a wife. Marrying older men was seen as a practical solution. Pre-marital sex, meanwhile, was strictly taboo—both culturally and religiously.

After their marriage, the couple discovered the man was impotent, which put a strain on their sexual relationship. The village dispensary didn't stock performance enhancement pills, and I knew suggesting alternative solutions could lead to me being ostracised. Left with no choice, I referred them to my supervisor, who was due to arrive in a few weeks. However, the couple never returned to follow through with the consultation when she finally arrived.

I graduated after my placement year and was handed two invitation cards for my convocation. It was a big moment for any medical student—taking the Hippocratic Oath and celebrating years of hard work. Naturally, I wanted to share it with the closest people in my life: Nida and Sufi's mother.

I couldn't manage an extra invitation for Sufi, convincing myself I'd visit him in person in the coming weeks and celebrate in our own way with Shiro and Rajesh. But that day never came.

You'd think that after enduring five gruelling years of medical school, everyone would want to use their hard-earned degree to do some good. Yet, I had female classmates who graduated, took their oaths, and then married wealthy men, abandoning their practice entirely for gossip sessions and tea parties. It was disheartening. If your intention is to become the smartest person at a tea party, there are other ways to achieve that without taking up a spot in a medical program—one that could've gone to someone committed to making a difference.

A few days after the graduation ceremony, I approached a visiting professor and introduced myself. This was in a time when important conversations were still held face-to-face, rather than relying on emails that might sit unread in someone's inbox or "Junk" folder—emails that an academic could ignore with excuses like "being too busy to respond". Anyway, the professor was a surgeon specialising in road traffic accident cases overseas and was looking for recent graduates to assist with a research project funded by a grant. I was eager for an opportunity to work with him and further my education. He explained that the project was deadline-driven and would kick off in just a month.

Most health professionals in Bangladesh choose service over research, as academia pays a fraction of what private practice can offer. Even those who enter academia often do so to secure tenure and add the title "Professor" to their credentials, boosting their credibility in practice. Rarely do people opt for pure research. Yet, I saw this as an opportunity—a stepping stone toward a potential PhD.

While I was clearly excited by the prospect, I remained conflicted in my mind. When I brought it up over the phone, Sufi's mother encouraged me to seize the opportunity. "We'll all be here when you come back—your family, Sufi, me, everyone. Now is not the time to hesitate," she reassured me. Nida shared in that sentiment.

With their support, I began preparing for the journey ahead after they left.

In the final days before my departure from Bangladesh, I received a call from Nida.

"You should talk to father one last time before you leave," she urged.

At that moment, I felt no fear toward him. Life had toughened me, and resentment toward him simmered beneath the surface for everything he had put us through. I snapped, "What's that going to change?" I could have simply said, "No," but deep down, I think I was fishing for Nida to convince me otherwise. I wanted my father to see the person I'd become now, almost as if to rub it in his face. I know, I know—classic *daddy issues!*

"He's been lucid for the last few days and opened up about things he never spoke about," she replied, a glimmer of hope in her voice.

It had been years since he became bedridden, gradually slipping into late-stage dementia. His lucidity now signalled a terminal phase—an unexpected and temporary improvement in cognition and memory that often occurs near the end of life.

"Great! 'Lucid' just means he's going to treat me horribly again. I'd prefer him as a vegetable," I retorted harshly.

Nida fell silent, then softly said, "He hasn't always been like that. Just talk to him before you leave, please. Do it for me!"

I sighed, annoyed, but ultimately agreed for her sake.

I made my way to her home, where she guided me to the room where she cared for our father. This was the first time I had seen him in years.

"I don't know how you've cared for him for all these years," I said.

"He's all I have," she replied, repeating her familiar mantra. "And I chose him, remember?" With a small smile, she sat him up in bed and guided his feet to the floor so he could face me. She continued, "If someone needs your help and you are able to offer it, you give it. We don't leave a person when they are in need because we reap what we sow."

"No one is born evil," Nida continued. The phrase struck a chord—I'd heard it before somewhere. "He's been going in and out of hallucinations, reliving a specific moment from his past."

I nodded, recognising the pattern. "Just like *Dadu*," I said.

Nida agreed, her expression sombre. "It seems to come with late-stage mental health disorders."

Her words lingered. "He was stuck in a particular time loop for years, but now, as he's more lucid, there's another layer added to it," she explained.

I was curious. "What time loop was *he* stuck in?"

Nida glanced over at our father, who remained fast asleep under his duvet, the fabric pulled up to his chin. He lay on his side, facing away from us, completely unaware of the conversation unfolding. After a moment, she looked back at me and began.

"Not a good one. It started with him describing how he was too weak to move, starving, as his armed captors threw him into the back of a truck."

"He was being carried around. Was this from when he was taken prisoner during the war?" I asked.

"Yes," Nida replied, her voice quiet but steady.

I stopped her. "Hold on, back up a moment. I was told he surrendered to a friend from Pakistan under civil terms and was taken back to Pakistan be tried for treason!"

Nida responded, "Yeah, some Brigadier. Father murmurs his name sometimes—Jawaad. He said there was a mutiny in Jawaad's camp after he surrendered: some of Jawaad's men couldn't stand him sharing meals with the enemy. They saw him as weak and stabbed him to death while he slept. Father held onto a silver neck chain that Jawaad had given him at some point in time."

I probed, "Do you think it's the same chain that's always been around his neck?"

Nida replied, "Maybe, but he couldn't tell me where it is. I think he lost it somewhere and now asks me repeatedly if I've seen it in one of his pant pockets.

Anyway, after the mutiny, instead of taking Father to back to face trial, they kept him with them. They had other plans for the war."

I frowned, trying to process it. "So, he was held captive by a band of deserters? Why lug him around? They'd already committed treason—what was the point of keeping him alive?"

Nida rolled her eyes. "I wasn't there, silly. How would I know? But if I had to guess, keeping a high-profile lieutenant could have been their bargaining chip in case they decided to surrender."

I refocused, realising we'd strayed off-topic. "Okay, so what else did he talk about in his lucid state?"

"He described how they intentionally starved him to prevent any resistance. He recounted a failed escape attempt, where his legs gave out and his captors found him with little effort. As punishment, they locked him inside a metal trunk on the back of their truck, a makeshift form of solitary confinement. For days, they fed him only peanut shells and leftover bones from their meals. Desperate, he rationed what little he had, hiding scraps in cracks and crevices within the trunk. As they drove across the countryside, raiding villages, the deserters abducted young women, tossing them onto the truck alongside him. His captors would have him bake in the sun throughout the day and in the evening throw him a single biscuit without water while they revelled in their spoils of war."

"Spoils of war?" I asked, though I already suspected the answer. I just needed to hear it to make sense of his torment.

Nida's eyes remained focused on mine. "Rape," she confirmed my suspicion. "They made him watch as they brutalised innocent, helpless women. He said that he would cry and beg them to stop, but they'd obviously ignore his pleas. He talked about hearing the women's screams, then gunshots after. He kept repeating how helpless he felt as he saw what happened around him in those makeshift rape camps."

"I can see why he might be stuck in that time loop," I replied, my curiosity deepening.

"He gradually became desensitised," she said, her voice now heavy with emotion. "He stopped pleading as they kept abducting and torturing young women. Instead, he would silently cry on the truck, his tears falling unnoticed while the men brutalised the women on the dirt roads. Over time, they lost interest in tormenting him. But one day, they picked up a beautiful young woman with a limp—likely a survivor of polio."

I listened intently as Nida recounted the story. "Father said he completely lost it. He cried, screamed, and struggled with every ounce of strength he had left, trying to protect her from the same fate he'd seen play out a hundred times before."

She paused, unsure whether I wanted her to stop. I nodded, silently encouraging her to continue.

"The captors were amused," Nida said, bitterness creeping into her tone. "They found it entertaining that he'd suddenly mustered the energy to fight back. In their twisted cruelty, they made him watch everything up close, taking extra time to torment her, knowing it would break him further. When they were finished, they tossed him and her lifeless body into the metal trunk and left them there together overnight. He spent the night weeping, clutching her as the hours dragged on. He said that everything after that was a blur. All he could recall was eventually being transported to a prison hidden deep inside a cave, though the details of how or when were lost to him."

Dadu, in the final stages of dementia, was trapped in a time loop, endlessly reliving the moment her son left for the army. She prayed for his return, clinging to the hope that he would rescue her from the tormentors who mocked her for her disability. Her son, meanwhile, was ensnared in his own time loop in his last stage—haunted by the memory of his failure to protect a handicapped woman from her tormentors. Such is the cruel irony of life: two souls reliving different moments of helplessness, yet each defined by the same enduring pain.

There are never winners in war, only losers. The stronger side dominates and imposes its will, often through unspeakable acts. Deserters and rogue operatives exploit their positions, breaking military codes of conduct to either stand up against injustice, or satisfy their darkest urges. These atrocities often occur under the noses—or without the knowledge—of the regimes they claim to serve. No war, no country, is exempt from this grim truth.

"You get the picture," Nida said softly, pulling me back from my thoughts. "Now talk to him. He's been asking about you a lot lately."

Gently, Nida moved to wake him. She roused him, helped him turn toward me, and propped him up to sit upright. With a reassuring glance at both of us, she said, "I'll leave you two alone to talk." Then, without another word, she quietly left the room, closing the door behind her, leaving my father and me alone in each other's company.

The years had not been kind to him. His hair had greyed, his skin was wrinkled, and the once muscular build had wasted away to a lean shell. His head trembled visibly, and he stared through clouded, unfocused eyes. For years, he had worn only simple home clothes; his favourite designer outfits were likely claimed by Ranjan. As I stared at him in silence, I realised that time and ill health are our greatest enemies.

Minutes passed in silence until he looked at me, seemingly in shock, as a tear rolled down his cheek. It was as if he were staring into a mirror, recognising a younger version of himself in me. He attempted to extend a shaky hand toward me, but it faltered. Then, as if he finally recognised me, he mumbled, "Yaad?"

I remained quiet, refusing to respond. He asked again, "Yaad, are you well?"

I met his gaze and replied with indifference, "Yes."

He studied me, struggling to articulate his next words. "I know I've caused you a lot of grief. I can remember some of it."

I watched him, feeling a mix of emotions as he continued, "I've been asking Nida every day to take me to see you one more time." A small smile broke through his pained expression. "I guess my last wish finally came true."

I leaned closer, unleashing years of pent-up anger. "You were the source of so much pain—grief, cries, and nightmares. You killed my mother with your abuse, traumatised me, and now you want me to re-live all that in your last moment of clarity?"

His gaze fell to the ground, almost ashamed, before he looked up again. "I've been living in captivity, haunted by those years, over and over. Your prayers have been answered, don't worry. I know I can nev-er take back what I've done, which is why I wanted to see you one last time." Another tear rolled down his cheek.

"To do what, exactly?" I asked.

"To beg for forgiveness."

I was taken aback by his admission. He continued, "I cannot justify anything that I have done. The only thing I can do is beg. Would you find it in your heart to forgive an old man and fulfill his last wish?"

As he sat there, I saw traces of the old man who used to sit on our driveway, wrapped in a shawl, hunched over but smiling as I handed him a penny. In that moment, I felt like that five-year-old again, but the joy I once felt now felt empty.

I was pulled back to reality as I saw him reach out, desperately ex-tending both arms in a feeble gesture to invite me for one last hug. "Please forgive me," he mumbled over and over.

What seemed like a simple phrase—"Yes, I forgive you"—felt im-possibly heavy in my throat. I couldn't bring myself to say it; hatred and resentment grew inside me as I faced him.

"Please!" he pleaded again, his voice tinged with desperation.

I drifted in and out of memories again from when I was five, watch-ing the old man who would sit on the driveway, quietly asking for alms. I'd eagerly offer him my tiny daily allowance, feeling a simple joy in the exchange. But here was frail Lieutenant Oman now, pleading not for money but for forgiveness—a currency without financial value. Strangely, I felt... nothing.

He lowered his outstretched arms, acknowledging my silence. Looking down in shame, he rubbed his left hand over his right, as if trying to console himself in a sad attempt to ease his own pain.

I met his clouded gaze once more, and he said, "I don't blame you for hating me. But I am very proud of how you turned out."

"It wasn't easy," I replied. "It still isn't."

He nodded feebly.

He lowered his head again in embarrassment, then lifted it back up, trying to muster a smile. "Nida said you're leaving and that I might not see you for a long time," he said, his voice tinged with a fragile hope.

"Yes," I replied, feeling the weight of finality in my words.

His expression darkened with sadness, a feeling that seemed genuine for the first time. "Then this is perhaps the last time we will see one another."

I felt a sinking sensation in my chest as I acknowledged the possibility. "Perhaps," I said.

I stood up and left the room, leaving the door open behind me. As I walked away, I glanced back to see him trembling on the bed, his gaze fixed on the floor.

Nida emerged from her room, concerned. "What happened? At least stay for dinner?" she asked.

"I have to pack. I'm sorry," I replied, feeling a mixture of guilt and resolve.

As I stepped outside, the last sound I heard from my father's room was the soft sound of him weeping.

I would soon leave Bangladesh, and my father would soon pass away from a heart attack with Nida by his side during his time of death. Kaushal sent me photos of Nida kneeling on the freshly turned earth of our father's grave—just as he had done years ago in front of *Dadu*'s grave, in the exact same posture. He had loved his mother, and in turn, his daughter loved him. It seemed so true: you reap what you sow.

I left behind loved ones to chase a dream: A collective dream. The hardest part about immigrating is leaving behind the ones who ground you, all for the hope of better opportunities. For me, that opportunity was perhaps the chance to tell my story.

After completing my Master's degree, I was awarded a full scholarship to pursue a PhD, bringing me one step closer to achieving a dream I once shared with someone dear to me. From that point on, everything seemed to align perfectly. I started working at a hospital, met a stand-up comedian who would later become my incredibly supportive partner, and now I have a life that most people back home could only ever dream of.

Looking back, there were definitely moments I should have handled better. I first sought out a counsellor for something unrelated, but he quickly pointed out that I had a treasure trove of 'interesting' unresolved issues. I'm still not convinced I agree with him on 'interesting', but hey, regular counselling turned into a delightful way to procrastinate on my PhD thesis and write a memoir! If he read this, I can just picture his reaction—he'd probably schedule an urgent session after realising I've spilled more tea here than in our sixty-minute chats, and that I might need to be institutionalised! Honestly, it wouldn't take much for him to convince anyone of that; all my counsellor would have to say is, "Good Heavens! The boy's lost it while doing his PhD," and my supervisor would nod sagely, as if that were a perfectly normal phenomenon and the most relatable thing in the world!

Now, I can practically hear him advising me to stop stalling and get back to my thesis. But don't worry, I'm all done with that and can confidently say that doing a doctorate was one of the best decisions of my life. I promised someone special that I'd make something out of myself and help as many people as I can along the way. In that regard, "*I have miles to go before I sleep*".

Now, let's address the elephant in the room. You might wonder if I've imagined parts of this story, given that dementia runs in my family. But that's exactly why I'm telling it now—before the memories fade. I understand why my counsellor suggested I write a book. Partly, it's a way to release my pent-up regrets and frustrations; partly, it serves as a record—a diary of key moments I might forget over time. And you know what? It works! That said, I can feel my memories slipping away, little by little, every day. Pursuing a PhD and making a series of questionable life choices hasn't exactly worked wonders for my mental health either.

In classic PhD fashion, I also managed to cut costs and save on copyediting my memoir by having my partner go through my drafts, making revisions to every section where she exclaimed, "I don't get it!" or "huh?" as she read along. When I was brainstorming titles for this book, I initially suggested something straight out of a researcher's handbook: "An Evaluation of Counselling Advice and Subsequent Reflections on My Past." Thankfully, my sensible partner shot that idea down before it could gain any traction with my colleagues in academia! She pointed out that I wasn't just writing about myself; I was also telling the stories of all the people who suffered in silence, exploited by their circumstances. So, this isn't just my story, it's a collective testament to those whose stories went unheard. Along the way, I got to share plenty of unpopular opinions— Probably enough to get me burned at the stake in the thirteenth century—or "*cancelled*" in the 21st, depending on which media outlet decided to run an exposé on me!

Part of mental health counselling is accepting the reality of what you've lost and learning to live with what you have. For me, that means acknowledging that Nida has started showing signs that she is heading down the same path as my father, convinced that everyone is out to get her! Despite my repeated advice to seek help, she brushes it off, I've come to terms with the grim reality that one day her condition will worsen beyond recovery. I could never give my mother the life she truly deserved, especially after she sacrificed so much for me. I'm sorry it took me so long to see the truth. This is why I prefer making choices in video games, where I can simply reload if things don't go my way.

Sufi's mysterious symptoms worsened and was later diagnosed with cancer while I was pursuing my Master's. We all came together to support him in any way we could. Nida even sold our car and used the money to contribute to Sufi's treatment. I visited him shortly after his surgery, and it was heartbreaking to see him struggling—he had lost his natural voice along with the salesman-like charm he'd always been so proud of. All I could do at that point was spend as much time with my friend as possible before work pulled me away again.

Shiro and Rajesh remained mostly unemployed and in between different jobs despite having a degree from a "prestigious school". Although, in reality, a degree is just a piece of paper, and experiences and useful professional connections matter more.

In the final stage of his illness, Sufi intentionally dropped off the radar, casually mentioning he was going to "meet a guy who knew a guy." Sufi remained a practical joker till the end with an unconventional view of the world. I will forever be grateful to him for revealing the darker side of the world to me—a complete stranger when we met—while shielding me from its harm and helping me pursue higher education. We figured he wanted to spend his final days in solitude with only his mother, close to Sammy, before joining her permanently. For the very few that asked about him, I told them that none of us went looking for him after he left; we knew he didn't want to be found.

Coming to terms with my own choices and outcomes has finally helped me realise that I am ready to read your story, Sufi. Thank you for entrusting me with it and choosing me to be the one to read it.

The last thing that my mother told me before she passed away was to not hold grudges. It wasn't a life lesson I took to heart at the time. But now I realise how silently holding on to bitterness eats at your soul, and you end up projecting that pain onto the people you love. I held a grudge against one man for far too long, and it turned me bitter.

Whether he deserved it or not is now irrelevant. Life catches up with us all, and maybe this story is my way of finally saying, "Yes, I forgive you."

Unpopular Opinions 2

"**I** am f*cked," I sighed, burying my face in my hands. "The bast*rd wrote things in his diary that make me feel like I should go back to Bangladesh, walk into a police station, turn myself in as an unwitting accomplice, go to trial, and plead insanity—because I still can't process how I got myself dragged into it!"

I was back in my counsellor's office after a year. He sat across from me, scrolling through his notes, clearly struggling to remember where we'd left off. "I wasn't expecting to see you again, Yaad. So... what did you find in your friend's diary?"

My eyes drifted to the cheap plastic hourglass on his desk. The sand clumped stubbornly at the neck, refusing to fall. Across the room, my counsellor was typing away on his keyboard furiously.

I tried answering his question while defending my deceased friend, fully aware that the contents of the diary could implicate a lot of people, including myself. "I found out that my closest friend had his reasons for what he did," I said carefully. "And now I understand why he went to such great lengths for me, teaching me so much about life. I just wish I could hug him and say thank you one more time."

But then, unable to hold it in any longer, I launched into a rant. "And you know what else I found out? My deceased friend was probably unhinged! *And* he was having these deep, thought-provoking conversations—with his inanimate diary!"

My counsellor gently interrupted, his tone calm but firm, he repeated his previous question. "What *exactly* did you find in that diary?"

I paused, inhaling deeply to collect myself. My hands instinctively fidgeted with the zipper of my bag on my lap, brushing against the top of the faux leather spine of Sufi's worn diary.

Sensing my hesitation, my counsellor looked at me and smiled. But it wasn't the comforting kind. It was the kind that made you feel like you were walking straight into a trap. "Read it for me," he said evenly.

Reluctantly, I pulled Sufi's diary out of my bag, set the bag on the floor, and placed the diary on my lap. I'd bookmarked the worst entries demonstrating Sufi's madness. Flipping to the first one, I hesitated.

"From the start, please," he interrupted.

I swallowed hard, nodding slowly. "Okay then... from the start."